FREAK OF NATURE

A novel by
James Ballou

© 2018, James E. Ballou
All rights reserved.
***3rd Revision, 2022**

This is a fictional story. If any names or other details featured herein have any likeness to those of real people or actual scenarios, they would be merely coincidental.

CHAPTER I

"Alright, Jessica, I am going to hold up one laminated card at a time from this stack in front of me and I would like for you to…"

"Tell you what is on the other side facing you," she interrupted. "But I already know what is on every card in that stack, so there is no need to hold them up one by one."

Dr. Holland was speechless. He stared at the four-year-old girl in disbelief, "How could you possibly know that?"

She shrugged her shoulders, "I just do."

He said he had to conduct the experiment, anyway, and test her incredible claim. He proceeded to show her the blank backside of each card one at a time, and she correctly described the images on the front of every card that she couldn't see. She didn't get a single one wrong.

"The most remarkable thing I've ever seen!" he said excitedly. "I want to conduct a few more tests."

Jessica Knowles remembered that morning thirteen years ago when her father took her to the mental research clinic for evaluation as if it were taking place right now in the present. She had been asked to participate in a variety of different test experiments.

At first, she considered it all too easy, the tasks that she was asked to accomplish. To an extent it was boring for her. But as the fascination over her unusual capabilities intensified and more specialists were summoned to witness some of the things her mind was capable of, she started to relish the attention.

She was smiling now just remembering it all. But things were much different now than they were then. In the present moment her gaze swept the roadside through the window of the moving Greyhound bus as her mind was retrieving memories of key events throughout her life, events that set her on this path. Some of these things – some of them were painful memories she knew she shouldn't dwell on.

Her destination was still more than a hundred miles further down the road. She would have another two hours on the bus to reflect on the past, and to contemplate this journey she'd set upon.

Despite the extraordinary power of her own mind, she had been feeling for a long time almost as though there was some external force carrying her to where she was going. It was a place she had never been to before and she hadn't consulted any maps at all, but she traveled with complete confidence as if she knew exactly how to get to precisely where she was going, and she knew everything that mattered about who she was going there to meet.

A woman traveling in the seat next to her was quiet, but Jessica could read what was in her mind. The woman's misery could not be kept private no matter how much she may have wanted to keep it private, at least not in the presence of Jessica, who couldn't always resist the temptation to get inside peoples' heads, and this was especially true whenever she was physically near a person.

From what Jessica could decipher the woman was traveling to Raleigh, North Carolina to see her sick and dying twin sister. She was also worrying about losing her job, for reasons that weren't revealed in her thoughts at the moment.

Jessica felt compelled to try to help the woman. She didn't want her to feel that her privacy had been violated even though in reality it had been, but the woman definitely needed help seeing her own life through a different lens, from a new perspective.

"Do you believe everyone is on his or her own unique and sacred journey in this life, Ma'am?" she asked her.

The woman appeared to have just awakened from a daydream. "Excuse me?"

"I mean, everyone has a different experience from everyone else for sure and, well, I believe we would all agree on that much. But would you say that these life experiences that each of us has - whatever they might be - that we were *meant* to have them and that everything that happens is for a purpose? Would you say we are all on the journey we were born to be on?"

The woman contemplated Jessica's question. "I'm not sure that's necessarily the case, but even if it were true how would any of us ever know for sure?"

"In my case I get this really strong feeling that the journey I'm on now appears to have been planned for me by a higher power," Jessica postulated, "probably before I was even born."

"You mean, by *God*?"

"Probably sounds ridiculous from a strictly logical perspective, right?"

"Oh, I don't know. I guess I've wondered about it like that before, too, but I've never seemed to be able to find the answer either way. I'll admit that I've never been a very religious person. It's just that so many things in this world seem so unfair. How could some of these things be allowed to happen to good people if there really was a God?"

"Maybe we're given challenges for reasons we can't understand. Maybe every single one of us has a more important role to play in this life than we realize."

The woman thought about what Jessica had said but didn't have a response. Jessica knew she had at least opened the woman's mind a little and got her to thinking. That was really all she had intended to do. The woman once again retreated into her own thoughts.

And once again with her eyes covered by sunglasses more to help hide her identity than to protect her eyes, Jessica gazed out the bus window. She noticed that a black, late model SUV was traveling alongside the bus in the inside lane and it suddenly pricked her attention. She remembered having seen the very same vehicle earlier in the day, many miles ago and in another town. She knew it was definitely the same vehicle because she remembered the number on the license plate. And she knew immediately that her seeing the vehicle again this far down the road was no coincidence.

Somehow, they knew she was on this bus. And somehow, they would also know her destination. They would be there waiting for her when she arrived.

And there was no doubt in her mind that they would, except that she wasn't going to be exiting the bus at the station on Person Street in Fayetteville like her bus schedule indicated. She decided immediately that the only intelligent course of action under the present circumstances would be to abandon this bus ride at the first rest stop before reaching Fayetteville, and then take a taxi cab from there, at least for a big chunk of the balance of her journey.

She was aware that there were other organizations besides certain agents within the federal government trying to kidnap her, and they all had different specific reasons.

Her senses correctly told her that certain elements in the federal government wanted her for scientific study because she was a natural phenomenon they couldn't explain or fully understand, but one that they felt they needed to understand (and also control) for national security purposes.

She had learned also that there were people in the Defense Department who actually wanted her destroyed because, at least in the minds of some of the higher ups at the Pentagon she could potentially present a threat to national security if she were to be captured and her powers exploited by some unfriendly foreign government or terrorist group.

And, of course, there were other organizations that also wanted to control and use her abilities for their own gain. The world she had long since learned to navigate through just to stay alive and remain free had become a daily obstacle course wrought with seemingly endless dangerous pitfalls. A person possessing any less mental capacity than she possessed, if pursued the way she was surely couldn't have remained free this long.

CHAPTER 2

"The Department of Homeland Security wants her just as badly as we do, Tony. That's just one more reason why our level of confidentiality absolutely has to be at its highest at all times. When we do finally take custody of this young lady and if somehow the feds learn that we've got her, you know as well as I do they'll be using every trick in the book to pry her away from us, and they'll be watching our every move until they see their chance."

Tony Byrnell knew that his boss, Brandon Carter, who happened to be the CEO and co-founder of the esoteric A.I. Technologies Corporation, was right about the need for airtight secrecy in this case. The firm's pet project, this nearly half a billion-dollar project, involved the development of artificial intelligence having a mental telepathy component.

The project had to be a closely guarded secret even within the compartmentalized organization, but a considerable amount of company resources nevertheless needed to be diverted to it, and they also needed a living, breathing entity that demonstrated the actual characteristics they were hoping to replicate, for testing and experimentation.

"Intercepting Jessica Knowles is proving to be quite a task, Mr. Carter," Tony said, "Certainly our allotted budget for private investigators is plenty generous and I'm confident that we've got the best people available tracking her movements.

"What we *do* know right now is that she bought a bus ticket to Fayetteville, North Carolina. But we don't know exactly why. She's been able to stay at least one step ahead of our people at every turn from the get-go. It's almost as if she knows exactly what people are going to do before they do it. In her case nothing would really surprise me."

Brandon Carter stood up out of his executive chair and walked over to the massive office window that had quite an impressive view of the city below.

"Well, we have to keep them on the task. When we started this enterprise fifteen years ago, we started with little more than a dream. This whole realm of parapsychology, as you well know, has long been viewed by the skeptical scientific community as pseudoscience and in our case nobody, at least nobody who has a reputation to protect would give us the time of day. We couldn't even get financing through conventional channels, but we didn't give up on it. Now look at what we've created – a billion-dollar corporation that basically owns the fields of both artificial intelligence *and* paranormal psychic phenomena.

"This happens to be our once-in-a-lifetime opportunity, Tony. During our careers you and I have both met more than a few who claim to be able to bend spoons or lift objects with only their mental concentration, but it's been a while since I've seen anybody actually do any of these things. Miss Knowles is the real deal. Her capabilities stretch beyond anything I've ever seen or even heard of before. She is a genuine freak of nature, and she's exactly what we need for our neurological replication."

"It's a real shame we can't simply offer her employment with A.I. Technologies, at least for this specific project we need her for. That would seem to be so much safer and simpler for everyone involved."

Brandon shook his head, "No, it really wouldn't be any simpler, especially not after what she's been through with her dad and everything that happened to *him*. We'd never get away with the kind of experiments we want to do while trying to follow fair employment practices at the same time. Besides, she doesn't need whatever salary we could offer her. You know her story. There'd be no real incentive for her to work with us in that capacity."

"I don't doubt that, but it's a shame, anyway. She's so young and so…"

"You gotta look at the bigger picture, Tony. I get what you're saying, I do. I feel the same way as you about all of this. But her contribution to mankind will be so much greater than that of almost any other single human being walking the earth right now, and we're here to help make that happen.

"Just look at it this way, everyone else who knows she exists is after her, too. If we were to miss out on this rare opportunity, someone else will eventually catch up to her and the outcome probably wouldn't be as good for her as what we plan to do."

"Are you confident that we can hold her after we finally have her in our custody?"

"Ketamine will help us with that. She'll be in a kind trance most of the time, at least as long as we need her to be. We can keep her sedated until we need her full mental capacity. Fortunately, we've got some of the best lab technicians in the country working for us, and all of them have the highest security clearances. They're definitely expensive employees, but they're absolutely essential to us. Of course, we've got to catch up to her first."

Tony stared into the eyes of his boss with a visibly somber expression when Brandon turned around. "What will we do with her after she's fulfilled our purpose?"

CHAPTER 3

Jessica paid the taxi driver his fare and also gave him a generous tip, and then exited the cab. She made her way across town carrying only her gym bag by its shoulder strap while managing to remain relatively inconspicuous. She knew she had more miles ahead of her, but she didn't want the taxi dropping her off any closer to her destination. She didn't want to leave behind a trail of her interactions with others that could potentially lead her pursuers anywhere near her destination.

Her only stop in town was at a sandwich shop where she bought a sub sandwich and a bottle of water. It had been hours since her last meal and she had by this time developed a ravenous appetite. The sandwich would give her the energy boost she needed as she continued on.

She didn't need to consult a map. She knew where she was going and her extraordinary intuition would guide her there. Wearing her sunglasses to hide her eyes and a cap on her head to help shield her face from any cameras or eyes in the air she crossed the city to the outskirts, and then followed a rural road into the country.

She had already walked at least a mile when an older model pickup heading in the same direction with its windows rolled down slowed almost to a stop as it rolled along side of her and the driver, a middle-aged woman, caught her attention.

"Hey there, girl, it looks like we're both headed the same way if you'd care for a lift."

Jessica looked at the woman and instantly sensed that she was trustworthy, so she unhesitatingly climbed into the passenger seat and thanked the lady for the ride.

"Do you have a specific destination?" the lady asked.

Jessica nodded, "It should be about six miles up this way according to my calculations, but I don't expect you to give me a ride that far."

"Well, I live on this road, almost exactly eight miles from that gas station back there, so it's on my way. My name is Carol, by the way."

"It's nice to meet you, Carol, and thanks again for the ride. I'm Jessica."

"Where're you from, Jessica? My guess is you're not from around the Fayetteville area, but you look kind of young to be in the Army, if you're stationed at Fort Bragg."

"That's a good guess. I'm not from around here and I'm also not in the military. I was born in Nevada, but I've moved a few times since then."

"What brings you here to North Carolina? Would that be one of your relatives who resides somewhere up this road?"

"We're not related. I'm actually on my way to a job interview."

"Hope you'll forgive me for all these questions, but it's not just every day I run into a young lady traveling on foot all by herself so far from home. What kind of work do you seek, Jessica, if you don't mind me asking just one more question?"

"Oh, I'm not the one who's going to be interviewed for a job. I just need help with something, and I know who can help me with it. But it's a little too complicated for me to try to explain it all right now, though."

The lady nodded, "That's all right. It's your business and I shouldn't be prying. I do hope it all works out for you."

Jessica was able to read Carol's genuine concern, and her curiosity. She wished she could share more of her story, and this lady's honesty and her friendly nature made doing so tempting, but Jessica couldn't ignore the risks involved with allowing others to know who she was. She didn't offer any more information about herself for the rest of the ride.

Before reaching her destination, Jessica had learned some things about Carol, too. From their conversation she learned that Carol lived on twenty acres and raised chickens and goats. But she also detected what Carol was presently focused on without much discussion, which was Jessica's well-being. The lady was genuinely concerned and even a little bit worried that the teenager might be in some kind of trouble.

As much as Jessica wanted to assure Carol that she had her own situation more or less under control, and as much as she knew she could trust this lady's genuine concern, she also realized that the fewer people who knew about her, the safer it was for everyone involved. And she had a powerful sense of that right now.

After she had been dropped off at the end of the long private graveled drive, Jessica knew immediately that Carol wasn't at all comfortable with leaving her there, and she could read the woman's sense of guilt for doing so. She was also getting a strong feeling that Carol's worries would somehow create complications at some point for her in the future, but she couldn't conceive of exactly how at the moment.

In any case she hadn't traveled all this way just to be distracted away from her course of action, and so she waved good-bye to Carol and started walking up the long driveway.

CHAPTER 4

About a fifth of the inside of the pole barn was separated from the rest of the building by a dividing wall with a door in the middle, and it was furnished like a studio apartment.

The modest but comfortable living space comprised a tiny kitchen area with a refrigerator, sink and countertop, a small bathroom, a deep closet, a carpeted concrete slab floor, insulated sheetrock walls and ceiling, a breakfast table and three chairs, a sofa, a single file cabinet, a dresser, and a bed. There was also a flat screen TV on one wall with a shelf supporting a DVD player with a collection of videos underneath it. Everything was kept neat and tidy. This end of the building that was separated from the main part was heated in the winter with a small woodstove.

The rest of the barn was open-framed and spacious. Suspended by a cable from a ceiling joist out in the open part of the building was a long, heavy punching bag over a large foam mat that covered much of the center of the concrete floor. Also suspended from the same joist but seven feet from the heavy bag at eye level was a small speed bag.

Along one of the inside walls were a couple of exercise machines and a weight bench. Hanging on pegs on one wall were a crossbow and several recurve bows, a compound bow, and dozens of arrows. There was also a gun safe just inside the door of the apartment's dividing wall.

At the far end of the building that had a gravel-covered dirt floor opposite the living quarters was a target backstop comprised of railroad ties stacked one atop another seven feet high behind a wall of sand bags stacked almost as high. In front of this backstop were several pistol and archery targets.

For the past two and a half years this barn had been Dugan Randall's residence and also his convenient personal training space. Until now the property belonged to his uncle for whom Dugan had worked part time as the property grounds keeper and residence maintenance man. That was how he earned his rent of the barn.

At twenty-nine years old Dugan was a uniquely and passionately driven individual. He had the look and physique of an Olympic athlete, and he possessed a high degree of skill in a variety of sports including mixed styles of martial arts, competition target shooting with everything from rifles, handguns, and shotguns, to traditional as well as modern archery.

He also possessed varying degrees of knowledge and proficiency in rock climbing, sky diving, swimming, off-road motorcycle riding, scuba diving, and wilderness survival. He had developed and refined his own lifestyle and training strategy since he'd gotten out of the Army, and nearly every waking moment of his free time had eventually become occupied by his series of self-challenges.

So many things in his world had lately been dramatically changing, though. His most recent primary employment had been as a security officer for a company that managed sports events and it was a job that paid well and entailed a considerable amount of traveling, which he craved. But that job disappeared a month ago when the company was acquired by another larger company that already had its own security contractors. He had been sending copies of his resume to a number of different organizations since then, but thus far no job offers.

The proverbial final straw on the camel's back came when he was informed by his cousin, Sarah, that her dad had agreed to sell the property, and Dugan would have to be moved out of his training paradise within thirty days.

The news caught Dugan totally off guard. He knew that his uncle's health had been failing fast in recent months and that the old man had already been moved to an assisted living facility for 24-hour special care, but he nevertheless kept hoping that the ranch would stay in the family, at least for the foreseeable future anyway. Now he was going to have to pack up and haul every bit of his training and exercise equipment to a storage unit in town until he could find a new place to settle into that could accommodate him and all of his equipment. And he realized that that could take a while.

He was trying to process all of these things when he heard loud knocking at the barn's apartment door. When he opened the door he was surprised to see a teenage girl with a gym bag slung by its strap over her shoulder. He couldn't help noticing how stunningly attractive she looked with her flowing auburn hair, large bright-blue eyes, and her delicate facial features, but she also appeared to be very young.

"Sorry Miss," he said, "I don't want to buy any Girl Scout cookies or magazine subscriptions or whatever else you might be selling today. Another day I might, but definitely not today. Thanks anyway."

"I'm not selling anything," she assured him before he had a chance to shut the door in her face. "You're Dugan Randall, right?"

He looked at her with a puzzled expression, "Yes, I'm Dugan. What can I do for you?"

"That lady up at the house told me I could find you here."

"Well, you've found me."

She looked him over carefully from head to toe and smiled, "Yes. I have, haven't I?"

"You have. Now, what is it that you want from me?"

"I'm here for a job interview."

"Job interview? I haven't been looking to hire anyone. What sort of work do you do?"

"No," she clarified, "I'm not looking for a job. I came here to interview *you* for a job."

He paused for a moment to consider what she'd said and then broke into laughter. She soon began laughing along with him.

"May I come inside where we can discuss business?" she finally asked after regaining her composure.

"Business," he echoed, turning more serious and also visibly curious. He reluctantly ushered her into his apartment and gestured for her to take a seat at his small breakfast table. "I can't wait to find out what kind of 'business' you're talking about. What grade in school are you in, Miss? Tenth? Eleventh grade maybe?"

She sat down as directed after lowering her bag to the floor next to her chair. "As a matter of fact, I've already finished high school and completed two semesters of college. I'd most likely be attending a university right now if I hadn't been forced to disappear. But my name is actually not 'Miss'. My real name is Jessica Knowles, although lately I've used other names on occasion in an attempt to throw the blood hounds off my trail."

"Oh, I think I understand what this is all about now," he said. "You're a runaway, right, and your family is trying to track you down? Unfortunately, I won't be able to help you at all with that one. You'll have to understand that I'm just not all that eager to take up residence inside a prison cell. How old are you, Jessica, sixteen maybe?"

"I'll be eighteen in a little over three months and besides, I believe the legal age of consent in North Caroline is 16, not that that has any relevance to why I'm here. My situation happens to be so much more complicated than you're assuming. I don't have any family trying to 'track me down'. My dad was my only family, and he was murdered last year."

He sighed, "Well, I'm sorry to hear about that. So, what did you want to hire me for, and why *me*? How do you even know who I am?"

"I know quite a bit about you, Dugan. I know that you sent a resume to the FBI last month and for reasons undisclosed they decided not to hire you, even though you're perfectly qualified for the position. I know that you reached the rank of Eagle Scout at the age of fifteen, and that you've earned multiple advanced degrees in several styles of martial arts and you've also worked as an instructor. I know that you served in the Army 5th Special Forces Group at Fort Campbell, and also a few years with the United States Special Operations Command at MacDill Air Force Base in Florida. I know that you were fairly successful as a private investigator before your most recent stint that paid even better working as a security officer with that sports events organizer. Too bad that job had to end, right?"

He looked dumbfounded. "How could you possibly know all of those things?"

She smiled, "I've done my homework. It wasn't too difficult to access the FBI's Personnel files and see the latest resumes that people had submitted. Yours intrigued me the most out of all of the ones I read, so I started doing more extensive research about you. In fact, I applied some of the same methods you've used for collecting information about people while you worked as a P.I."

"Well, I don't know whether I should be unnerved by that revelation, or impressed instead and even flattered by it. Anyway, in what sort of capacity did you want me to work for you?"

"My life is in danger and I need a 24-hour body guard, at least until I can establish an air-tight criminal case against the people who killed my dad, or if nothing else at least severely disrupt their operations."

"Why was your dad killed?"

"They killed him because he refused to help them find me."

"First, I need to know who 'they' are, and second, why are they trying to find you?"

"Okay, this is where it gets a bit complicated. It could take me a while to explain it all. Can we go somewhere for lunch? I'm getting hungry."

"You're suggesting that I take you into town where I nearly always run into someone I know, and risk being seen out in public with a girl who looks younger than seventeen (with me pushing thirty), and buy you lunch just so you can decide whether or not I'm the right person for this job of yours?"

"Yes, that's more or less what I'm thinking, but we could go to a drive-through fast-food place where there's little chance of anyone recognizing you or noticing me, and I'll be wearing my dark sunglasses anyway. I was actually planning to treat you to lunch, though, as long as you drive because I don't have a car. I've done quite a bit of walking today and I've been working up an appetite. Besides, I've already decided that you're the right one for the job."

"What if I decline your job offer?"

"You won't decline."

"How do you know I won't? What does this job pay, anyway? No offense, Jessica, but you don't look like someone who could pay my required salary."

She lifted her bag off the floor and set it on the table in front of her, retrieved an orange envelope from one of the side pockets and handed it to Dugan. He opened the top flap and briefly glanced inside to see the thick bundle of fifty-dollar bills.

"It's a week's pay in advance, cash under the table so as to avoid a paper trail," she said, "Seventy President Grants, or thirty-five hundred dollars if you prefer to think of it that way. You can count it right now if you want to.

"So," she continued, "I'm offering to pay you five-hundred a day for your services, which I believe is five hundred more than your income happens to be at the moment, or at least while you've been unemployed. But we'll have to do a bit of traveling and you'll be driving, so I will also pay all of your fuel expenses, as well as our meals and hotel fare while we're on the road."

He glanced up from the envelope and looked her in the eyes, "You are definitely serious about this, aren't you, Jessica?"

She nodded, "I *have* to be serious, Dugan. My journey is a treacherous one. Make no mistake about it - this is a very dangerous job you're taking on."

CHAPTER 5

Carrying an oversized leather-covered briefcase with a titanium inner shell, Walter Hayworth entered the office occupied by his boss, General Douglas Chase, who was presently the Director of the National Security Agency. Walter left two of his own armed security guards posted outside the door, but nobody else happened to be in the office besides the two of them, and Walter closed the door behind him. The briefcase contained a thick stack of sensitive hardcopy documents.

Walter was cognizant of the sensitive nature of the material in his possession and he took appropriate precautions in handling it, though he also had a sense that his own security clearance probably warranted an updated review for official authorization to handle what the briefcase contained in this instance. If his team were ever pressed by Congress's oversight to provide a full report on their procedures in this case he knew it would raise plenty of questions and focus a lot of unwanted attention on the agency. That made him feel a little bit uneasy, although he was very good at not showing it.

This was an unprecedented and rapidly evolving situation, however, and not all of the critical details about determining things like the appropriate clearance levels and authorized methodologies had yet been entirely sorted out. Those in charge in this case tended to follow the wisdom that it was better to err on the side of safety for the nation.

In the meantime, Walter's duty was to report to the general and he knew that the information he had been burdened with needed to make its way up through the appropriate channels without delay. He also knew that if the public were to ever learn about the NSA's use of human intelligence as it was doing in this case with the knowledge of the Director, outside their official realm of signal intelligence, there would be repercussions.

But General Chase was repaying a favor to an old friend and he was in the process of putting together a complete and detailed report for the Secretary of Defense, and there was no question in anyone's mind who was involved in this mission that this was a matter of critical national security that warranted bending whatever rules might be necessary in order to gather the necessary Intel in a timely manner. General Chase had a reputation for accomplishing missions at all cost, even if it meant playing outside some of the rules.

Walter set the briefcase on his boss's desk and gave him the combination to its lock, then took a seat in one of the chairs in front of the general's desk.

"No digital copy of it exists anywhere, Sir," Walter assured his boss, "I can confirm that much. The author of this paper, Dr. Lyle Richardson is a renowned psychologist and leading authority in the field of parapsychology, and he is one of just a few to have observed the Prodigy first hand and to have kept several years' worth of notes about her, and now he understands the gravity of it. The two of us had a long talk, under the FBI's supervision, of course. He's got a daughter currently attending college and I painted him a grim picture of her future – along with that of all of the rest of us - if his research on this matter happened to find its way into the public domain and ultimately the wrong hands."

"How much certainty can we have that no part of the doctor's notes pertaining to this subject were sent to Popular Science, or to one of the other science journals in his queries for pitching his paper?" the general asked.

"On that the certainty is irrefutably one-hundred percent, Sir. Rob Haley is among NSA's best IT men and at my request he spent eight hours digging through Dr. Richardson's computer files. No piece of hidden data in any computer can elude Rob. If there were such a thing as being *too* thorough, then it would be precisely how we would describe Rob."

"And, of course, you would have seen to it that he's been cleared for this mission, correct?"

"Yes Sir. As you might remember, Rob previously worked for DIA. His clearance level since he started working for us has been upgraded from Secret to Top Secret.

"The truth is, Sir, we owe Rob full credit for discovering the existence of this research paper in the first place. And everything he's found related to the Prodigy - and not just in Dr. Richardson's computers but also in every other computer belonging to anyone and everyone we suspect has had the opportunity to observed and study the Prodigy - all of their notes and data are now inside this briefcase in printed form, all nineteen hundred and seventy-nine pages in condensed text format, and the electronic files have all been permanently deleted. In addition, all of the computer hardware devices that we searched are now safely locked up in our secure storage facility, under twenty-four hour guard service provided by the United States Army's Military & Police."

"Good work, Hayworth. Your diligence in following the security protocols will help every one of us connected to this operation sleep much easier at night."

"Thank you, Sir. But I can tell you that I probably won't be sleeping too easy as long as the Prodigy remains outside the scope of our protection and complete control."

"Good people are working on that," the general said. "Norquist over at Homeland is in charge of that end of it – the matter of securing the Prodigy. He can act on the Intel we send him, and he's got his task force and all the resources he needs at his disposal. This young lady will eventually come up somewhere on the radar screen and when she does he'll be one-hundred percent ready to mobilize his team at the drop of a hat."

 The general then opened a drawer in his desk and retrieved a flask of Captain Morgan Spiced Rum, along with two shot glasses. He set the glasses on his desk and poured rum into both, then handed one to Walter.

 "Each of us from different departments assigned to this operation, Hayworth, was handed his responsibilities for good reason and we can rest assured that each executes his own duties to the fullest of his own capacity - just as you've done, and it helps if we periodically remind ourselves that the others on our same side are doing their part the same as we're doing ours."

 Walter raised his glass before taking a sip, "To DHS's success in keeping the Prodigy out of foreign hands, Sir!"

 The general also raised his glass, "Indeed! To making sure of it, and to keeping this great nation safe!"

CHAPTER 6

Dugan and Jessica ordered eight hard shell tacos to go at a Taco Bell drive-thru in Fayetteville, and then found a somewhat shaded parking area not far away where they could sit in his Jeep and eat their lunch.

He asked her a lot of questions while they ate and she didn't hesitate to answer them all, and she answered them in considerable detail. She understood even more clearly than he did the requisite that he be fully apprised of her unique situation.

"Okay," he said finally, "if I'm going to take your money for this job then I want to make it clear that we'll be doing things my way and you'll have to trust my methods."

"Deal," she agreed without hesitation. "There is one small detail you didn't think to ask me, though, but I think you should nevertheless be aware of it since we'll be working so closely together."

"What is it?"

"I can read peoples' minds. Every thought you have, you might as well be whispering it right into my ear."

He looked at her in disbelief, "You can really do that? Is that even possible in the real world?"

She nodded.

"Okay then, tell me what I'm thinking right now," he looked around, searching for something to focus his attention on nonchalantly before pausing to concentrate on it.

"You have two separate lines of thought running through your mind right now," she informed him after chewing and swallowing a bite of taco and then wiping her mouth with a napkin she retrieved from the paper bag. "You're wondering with a lot of skepticism if the ability to read someone's mind could actually be a real thing (and I wouldn't even have to read your mind to know that), and at the same time you're trying to focus your attention on that gray pickup that's parked facing the building on the other side of this parking lot. You're debating what color you would prefer it to be if you owned it."

He looked stunned. He had just taken a bite of a taco and suddenly his chewing stalled nearly to a halt while he contemplated her answer.

"Then what color am I favoring?"

"You're thinking about how cool that truck would look with a custom paint job in turquoise with chrome bumpers and a chrome grill, but at the same time you can't ignore the advantages of a more subtle, sort of generic color like white or maybe its own silvery-gray that tends not to stand out among other vehicles in traffic. You are keen on the benefits of avoiding drawing attention to yourself. You prefer blending into the crowd."

He nearly choked on his food, "How are you able to do that? I never knew that anyone could actually do things like that – in movies, sure, but not in real life. That's just crazy! You're psychic!"

"It's what I've been telling you. But I'm not just some mystic or some palm-reader psychic. I have mental capabilities that others don't have, or at least I've never known of anyone else who could do what I can do. It's as simple as that, and it's why I'm being hunted like an exotic rare wild creature, just like I said."

"I think you *are* an exotic rare wild creature, Jessica."

"Ha! Ha! Funny! But don't forget, I already know what you're thinking."

"What else are you able to do with your mind?"

"Throw me a random mathematical problem if you want," she said, "but nothing easy. You can check my answer with that calculator in your smart phone."

"I'm surprised you don't have your own smart phone," he said. "I have a cousin who's fifteen I think and she's always on her phone it seems. I thought all young kids were like that."

"Computers and digital handheld devices are all plenty useful when you need to send texts or emails or look something up," she admitted, "and naturally I can't process everything as quickly as a machine, but I've just never felt the need for one."

He gave her a long stare, "No, I don't suppose you would. Okay, let's see, how about… six hundred and eighty-three times two hundred and forty six?"

"Oh, that's way too easy! How about a hundred and sixty-eight thousand, eighteen?" she answered without even pausing to mentally calculate it. "I was expecting a much more complex equation to solve."

He checked her answer on his phone and then shook his head in amazement.

"You can throw me another test if you want," she boasted, "quiz me about anything you can possibly think of."

"No need, I think I've seen enough for now to be convinced. It might take me a while to completely process it, though. How many people know about this, about what you can do?"

"Too many people know now, and that's why my life is in a constant state of danger. Elements in the United States government consider me a potential threat to national security because if some terrorist organization or another nation that maybe isn't friendly to the U.S. were to capture me they might force me to use my abilities against my will – they'd most likely try to use me as a weapon. And then there are some in the technology industries who want to exploit my abilities for their own purposes. Honestly I wish nobody knew about me – about my mental capacity."

"For how long have they known about you?"

"My dad took me to see a cognitive scientist before I was even old enough to start elementary school, mainly because he wanted to determine whether or not I was an autistic savant. It was determined that I was not, of course, but soon I started receiving a lot of attention from the medical and science communities. Our lives – mine and my dad's - suddenly got really complicated after that."

Dugan chewed and swallowed another bite of his taco and then nodded, "Well, you've obviously managed to stay alive and remain free all this time without any help from me, so I'm not exactly sure how I could be of any use to you now."

She shook her head, "While it is true that my brain capacity was deemed by the psychologists who've examined me to be far beyond any human norm, which is really more of a curse than any sort of blessing, I am nevertheless only human, Dugan. I don't have the years of training in martial arts and self-defense like you have, or worked in security jobs like you have, or served in the military or ever had any experience with weapons or covert operations or any of that kind of stuff. If I weren't absolutely convinced that I needed to employ your skillset, then I wouldn't have traveled this far to recruit your help."

"Fair enough," he replied with a nod, "I just didn't want to be taking your money unnecessarily. And I realize that this *is* a lot of money for a teenager to be shelling out. It's probably all or most of your life's savings, am I right?"

"Well, not exactly. Right now money is the least of my concerns. When my dad was alive, I could tell him which stocks were the most lucrative to invest in, which horses to bet on at the races, where and when to buy the winning lottery tickets. He raked in gobs of cash over the course of just a few years.

"But he always anticipated the day when he and I might be forced to go on the lam and then we'd need access to paper currency without the possibility of it being electronically traced. So he squirreled away bundles of fifty-dollar bills in small quantities over a period of time to avoid drawing any attention. I believe I still have more than a thousand of those fifties left in my bag here that I've been carrying around with me, and I know where a whole lot more are safely hidden. So I won't be running out of money anytime soon."

Dugan raised his eyebrows, "That's handy, all right. I just might end up having to marry you for your vast wealth someday," he said jokingly, "*After* you turn eighteen, of course."

"Oh, of course!" she played along with his humor, adding her own dose of sarcasm, "A child like me who still plays with dolls and scribbles with crayons simply wouldn't be ready for that type of a commitment. I agree it's just so much better to wait another three and a half months - until I grow up - before buying myself such a sensitive and caring husband as you, with my riches."

He couldn't keep from laughing at her witty comeback. He wadded up his empty taco wrapper and stuffed it into the paper sack, now serving as a trash bag.

"Where can we find these people who killed your father?" he said after a moment of quiet contemplation, watching her finish eating.

"There is a very ruthless and powerful crime ring operating out of Miami that, among other criminal enterprises engages in human trafficking internationally," she said, "They've remained untouchable for quite a while. The FBI did manage to have one of their agents infiltrate the organization last summer, working to put together a solid case against them when somehow that agent's cover was blown. They were able to move their "cargo" (the people they were holding against their will) to a different location before a search warrant could be obtained, and that FBI agent was murdered - murdered the same way my dad was. The FBI still has no prosecutable case against them.

"Meanwhile, the leader of that organization is convinced he has an overseas buyer willing to pay handsomely for me. I know it sounds totally insane but the incentive for finding and grabbing me in this case is a huge pile of money, like a multi-million dollar deal. My dad suffered a horrible death as he was unwilling to help them all the way to the bitter end."

"Your dad sounds like an incredible man."

"He was. He gave his life trying to protect mine."

"How did you find out all of these details about that organization?"

"The same way I've learned everything I learned about you, Dugan - through research."

"Impressive! Maybe I should start up a new private detective agency, and hire *you*."

"You know you could never afford me," she said, smiling.

"I guess that's true. Looks like I'll just have to get used to working for you instead of the other way around."

"You're still in charge, though," she reassured him, "I did agree to your terms on that. I know what needs to be done, but we'll do it your way."

"Perfect. Then we'll pack a few suitcases for a road trip to Florida and we'll put a stop to their activities. But before we embark, I think you could use a couple days of training. Fortunately, I'm a certified instructor."

CHAPTER 7

Jessica's first lessons in self-defense had commenced in the barn almost immediately after they had returned from lunch. Dugan was mindful of her eagerness to get on with her mission but he wanted to make sure she was physically as well as mentally (and psychologically) prepared for it, or at least as prepared as she could become in such a short period of time.

The application of lethal force when applied even in justifiable circumstances such as self-defense, he explained, can bring internal psychological turmoil with long lasting consequences. He wanted her to grasp the nature of those skills he was about to train her in, and the gravity of the path she had already embarked on. Until now her only defensive equipment, besides her unmeasurably powerful mind, consisted of a single small can of pepper spray. After today she would become potentially much more dangerous to her adversaries.

Using a rubber model of a Glock 17 pistol as a training prop, he taught her some effective close-quarters blocking and take away techniques. He had her practice the moves over and over until he was confident that she could execute them safely and effectively within the blink of an eye.

Next, he showed her how to load and shoot a variety of handgun types, from a snub-nosed double-action revolver to several different styles and sizes of auto pistols. He noticed right away how quickly and intuitively she learned new information and skills, and she seemed to be retaining what she learned extraordinarily well during her first lesson.

The simplest hand-to-hand moves would require considerable practice, however. She weighed a hundred pounds or slightly less, but her natural swiftness and her ability to read the thoughts of others and apply the element of surprise would give her a healthy advantage. On the sparring mat Dugan found her to be a formidable opponent.

"Okay," he said finally after two and a half hours of continuous and intense training, "it's time for an hour break for dinner and to re-charge our batteries before we watch some videos on lock picking techniques and how to break out of handcuffs. I've got plenty of frozen dinners in the freezer. We can heat up some of those fairly quickly and most of them are filling, if not necessarily all that tasty. After that it's back to the training."

"Hmmm..." she uttered, "handcuffs, huh? That sounds kinky."

"Yeah, I guess it does, doesn't it? And just wait 'til you see my collection of different products! But seriously, after you watch some of these videos and practice the techniques, you'll be able to escape from any type of handcuffs. We'll also practice some methods of defeating zip ties tightened around your wrists and even duct tape and rope bindings. These Houdini tricks could be life-saving skills for someone in your shoes, trust me."

Not long after sundown Jessica and Dugan were both physically exhausted and ready for a good night's rest. He let her have his bed and he slept on the floor in a sleeping bag. If either of them snored in the night, the other would have been too deep in their sleep to have heard it.

Jessica woke up the next morning just before sunrise to the sizzling sound and the aroma of bacon frying. Dugan was already up and making breakfast, which consisted of scrambled eggs, fried bacon, and toasted slices of wheat bread.

"That smells inviting," she said, sitting up in the bed and rubbing her eyes, "but what time is it?"

"Well good morning, Sleeping Beauty! It's a little bit past five-thirty. We've got quite a day ahead of us." His mind was the clearest and his body was the most rested and ready for action in the earliest part of each day, he informed her.

She watched him as he stirred the eggs in the pan over the stove, the tiny kitchen space of this studio apartment being only about fifteen feet from the foot of the bed with no walls in between.

"I know all about the plan you're cooking up in your head, Dugan."

He suddenly looked at her with surprise, "The plan I'm 'cooking up'?"

She nodded, "You're thinking about how we might be able to get that human trafficking ring I told you about busted and shut down for good if we could simply free some of their victims and convince them to tell everything they know to the authorities."

"So, for how long have you been eves-dropping on my thoughts this morning?"

"'Eves-dropping'? I warned you yesterday about that, about what I do. It's not something I can just turn off and on that easily, you know. Did you think I was kidding when I said you might as well be whispering all your thoughts directly into my ear?"

"Well then, if you've been reading my brain then you know I don't have any of the details of my 'plan' sorted out just yet. I've merely been considering different possibilities. But anyway, what do you think of this one idea that I've been kicking around mainly?"

"I'd definitely give you high marks for your strategy development, but I think your plan still needs serious revision. The way you're contemplating going about it at this point seems too dangerous to me. Oh, I haven't forgotten that I agreed we're going to do this your way, and I'll stick to my agreement. I'm just saying that if they were to catch you in the process of trying to separate them from their merchandise, they would kill you for sure, and I never wanted to recruit your help just to get you killed."

"Then I'm all ears for hearing the details of your plan."

She paused to think before offering her own ideas.

"I think the basic principle of your strategy – at least that part about rescuing some of their victims and delivering them to law enforcement – seems like a logical idea," she admitted, "And even though it wouldn't be making these criminals accountable for my dad's murder directly, it *would* most likely put these evil people behind bars for a very long time and severely impede the Miami sex slave trade. That might be the best we can hope for.

"But there might be a more reliable and safer way to make that happen than trying to break into one of their secure facilities," she continued, "Even if we *did* manage to free some of their prisoners against the odds, as soon as the organization discovered their security had been compromised, they would immediately move their merchandise to a new, possibly even more secure secret location. After that it could be next to impossible to breech their shield ever again."

"Then how should we go about it?"

"My extraordinary brain is on task with that, Dugan. But that breakfast you're fixing smells so good and I'm so hungry! I might have to eat before I can think straight."

He loaded a plate and grabbed a fork and a napkin, then brought them to her while she was still in bed.

"Hmm, breakfast in bed? What a nice treat!" she remarked with a grin. "I think I could actually get used to this."

"I'll bet you could," he said, "but I wouldn't get too used to home cooked meals right now. When we're out on the road we'll have to make do with whatever is the fastest and most convenient."

Jessica hadn't even taken her first bite of the breakfast when Dugan was distracted by what he saw through the barn's tiny kitchen window. The small window had a view of the house and the graveled drive around the front of it, and he saw a black SUV drive up and park near the front door, then two men got out and stepped up onto the front porch.

"Two guys just drove up the driveway in a black SUV and parked over by the house," he said. "It looks like they're knocking on the front door. Sarah probably hasn't left for work yet. Jeez, it's not even six o'clock yet! They'll no doubt be asking her all the important questions."

"Carol!"

"Say *what*?"

"The lady who gave me a ride up this road and dropped me off near the end of your long driveway yesterday, her name is Carol. She was so worried that I might be a runaway, even though I did my best to reassure her that I'm not a runaway. I mean, her concerns were genuine enough and she meant well and everything, but I'm afraid she inquired with local law enforcement about recent reports of runaways. When she described me to them, her inquiry must've red-flagged the feds. They sure do get an early start in the morning on a new lead, don't they?"

"Sarah will send them over here to the barn no doubt," Dugan mumbled, pulling himself back from the window out of view from outside, "The only good place for you to hide I believe would be in my closet. When they get here, I'll try my best to talk them off your trail."

She did as he suggested and, after handing Dugan her plate of untouched scrambled eggs and bacon with the fork and napkin, she hastily kicked her daytime clothes under the bed out of view and then disappeared into his closet still wearing only her pajamas. A moment later there was knocking on his door.

From inside the dark closet she could hear the dialogue. She could also mentally envision the characteristics and read the thoughts of both men. One was taller than the other, and the taller man did most of the talking.

"Sorry to bother you this early in the morning, Sir," the taller man said, retrieving his identification from his pocket to show Dugan. "I am Agent Nathan Curry with the Department of Homeland Security, and this is my partner, Agent Scott Hauser. Are you Dugan Randall?"

Dugan nodded, "Yes, I am. How can I help you gentlemen?"

Agent Curry produced a small photo from his shirt pocket and showed it to Dugan, "We're looking for this girl, and the lady up at the house said she came by here yesterday. Do you know where she is?"

Dugan studied the photo briefly and then looked at the two men, "She said her name was Jessica and that she wanted to hire a bodyguard. She must've done an Internet search and run across my name as someone who's worked as a security guard – she wouldn't offer much in the way of an explanation about that, however. I thought she seemed paranoid about something and I wondered what kind of trouble she was in, but I just figured that was really her business and not mine.

"Anyway, when she realized that I wasn't available for hire she asked me if I would give her a ride back to town. So that's what I did. I dropped her off as she requested at the bus station on Person Street. I didn't want her to have to walk that far. It's easily at least twelve miles or more from here."

"May we come inside and talk with you about those details for just a few minutes?"

Dugan shrugged his shoulders and then motioned for them to step inside. He gestured for them to take seats at the small breakfast table, and they did as he directed.

"You guys hungry at all? I cooked up quite a mess of bacon and eggs. Not sure I'll be able to eat it all."

"None for me, Mr. Randall," Agent Curry said, "We've got a lot of ground to cover in a limited amount of time. But thank you for the offer anyway." Agent Hauser shook his head and also thanked Dugan for offering.

"Did she say where she was headed to from that point?"

"No, she wouldn't tell me. I asked her about that but all she said was that it was better for me if I didn't know anything. So I didn't bother her about it again. What is this all about, anyway? She didn't really look like a terrorist to me at all. Maybe a runaway – she wouldn't even tell me how old she is, but she's definitely not a terrorist."

"We're not at liberty to discuss any of the details. But you've been very helpful to us, Mr. Randall, and we appreciate you taking the time to talk with us this morning. I'll leave you a phone number where either I or Agent Hauser can be reached and if by chance she returns here please do call us."

"You bet. Hopefully you can access the bus's passenger log if they maintain something like that or maybe find a witness around the station. I've worked as a private investigator among other things and I've tracked people down on occasion so just let me know if there's anything else I can do to help."

While she remained as still and silent as anyone could be crouched down on the floor of the dark closet right next to a guitar case, Jessica detected Dugan's worry after he noticed her bag had been unknowingly left out in plain sight by the bed. He was trying not to allow his paranoia to distract him, worrying that one of the federal agents might notice it and possibly recognize it as belonging to her. But she could also read their thoughts and she knew that it hadn't registered with either of them.

Agent Hauser's attention *was* drawn to Dugan's sleeping bag, however, which was rolled up and sitting on the floor next to the wall across the room.

"Isn't that one of those U.S. military-issue down-filled mummy bags?" he said. "At least it definitely has that olive drab color to it. In my experience those things are hard to beat. If you don't mind me asking, how much did you have to shell out for it?"

"Oh, yeah, it's genuine government-issue. Excellent bags," Dugan agreed, and Jessica could sense his feeling of relief and consolation in the fact that he had taken the time to roll it up right after he'd gotten up less than an hour earlier, now suddenly thinking that it would have been rather awkward trying to explain an open and apparently just-used sleeping bag on the floor in the same apartment with an unmade bed. "I happened to score on this one at an army surplus store in Fayetteville last year. I think it was fifteen bucks in that closeout sale they were having. It's a fairly heavy bag for mild weather and occupies a lot of room in my pack, but sometimes it's well worth it. I was cleaning out my closet and got that out to clean it."

"Can't beat that price," Agent Hauser replied.

"What's the rest of this building used for?" Agent Curry asked, looking curiously at the door separating the apartment from the main part of the barn.

"I've mostly been using it for a workout gym and indoor archery range. It's been super handy for helping me keep fit and my skills honed. Would either of you gentlemen care to test your skill at launching a few arrows this morning?"

Agent Curry stood up from his chair, and then Agent Hauser did the same. "As much as we would probably enjoy that," Agent Curry said, "we better get back on track pursuing that lead that you've given us. The more time we spend here, the less chance we'll have of catching up with her. Besides, you should probably eat your breakfast while it's hopefully still warm."

"I understand perfectly," Dugan said, "Maybe another time then."

The federal agents thanked him again for his time and the information and then left.

Dugan locked the apartment's front door deadbolt behind them and watched through the little kitchen window as they strolled back up the driveway and got into their vehicle before making his "all clear" announcement. Jessica then emerged from the closet cautiously, still in her pajamas.

"There for a little while I was wondering if you were going to invite them to stay for dinner!" she said facetiously.

"Well I didn't exactly want to give them any reason to suspect I might be hiding their fugitive in here. You know as well as I do these guys are trained in reading peoples' reactions and mannerisms. Better to come across as relaxed and willing to help their efforts as opposed to appearing annoyed or worried."

She nodded, "Yeah, I know. All jokes aside, I do appreciate the way you handled them, which was pretty clever I'll admit. I owe you my gratitude."

He shook his head, "I figure I should actually be earning all that money you're paying me."

"So now do you see what I've been talking about? People *are* really after me - you can see now that I'm not simply delusional!"

"You're right. Your ridiculously unbelievable story has now been upgraded to believable. I never expected a visit like that this morning and especially this early in the morning, that's for sure."

"So can we finally eat our breakfast now? Lucky for us those guys didn't hear my stomach growling from inside the closet!"

He set her plate in the microwave just to warm it up for thirty seconds while he dished up a plate for himself. While they ate their breakfast, they revisited the subject of their "plan". Now that she'd had a little while to consider things, Jessica's brain was able to concoct a fairly intricate plan and contemplate most of the potential pitfalls.

They heard another car driving over the gravel on the driveway and Dugan quickly peered out his kitchen window to investigate.

"Oh, it's just Sarah leaving for work. Her shift starts pretty early."

"I wonder what she's thinking about me spending the night in here. I haven't even thought about getting inside her head yet."

"Oh, Sarah never seems to be terribly concerned about my personal life or what I'm up to most of the time, but I'd actually be surprised if she even knows you're still here."

"That would be the best thing - the fewer people who know who I am and where I am, the better."

Jessica then shared a brief synopsis of her idea with Dugan and he listened quietly, then expressed skepticism and finally admitted that he needed some time to process all of it.

CHAPTER 8

"I had a thought," Jessica shared, "When we get to Miami you could pose as an opportunistic chemist trying to secure funding for the development of a new drug that you could claim has many of the same attractions to druggies that meth has, but without most of the nasty side effects, or maybe even some type of counterdrug. I could pose as the commodity you have for sale, to secure the funding your project needs. Part of the deal might even include releasing a few of the prisoners to your custody, since you'll need subjects for your own drug testing. Like I said, I am a valuable prize in the human trafficking market."

His initial reaction was exactly what she had expected it would be. His facial expression was one of skepticism. "These things rarely ever go exactly as planned," he warned, "but if even one single phase of such a plan were to fail everything could go horribly bad for either you or me, or for both of us."

"To safely pull it off you'll have to be convincing, that's for sure," she countered, "Just like you were with these two men this morning, though I know you were having some internal conflict with that. I could sense that deception doesn't come naturally to you, which I actually consider a credit to your character as a human being."

"Thanks, but I don't believe deception is a natural thing for hardly anyone, really. But some people are obviously easier with it than others."

After they'd finished eating their breakfast and she'd gotten herself dressed and stuffed her lightweight pajamas back into her gym bag, they went into the main part of the barn to resume her training. To his astonishment she not only remembered every detail of all that he had taught her the day before, but she had become even more proficient, and faster. Faster answering his test questions, and faster in the execution of her newly learned moves and skills.

On the pistol target she put two cylinder loads from Dugan's Ruger SP101 revolver all into the bull's eye ring at fifty feet, shooting double-action, and then she almost perfectly repeated this same performance with both his 1911 45-caliber pistol and also his 9mm Glock 17, throwing only two rounds barely outside the ring out of two magazine loads for each pistol. She also demonstrated impressive speed with the cylinder reloads in the revolver and with the magazine changes of the auto pistols.

"Damn, Girl! You weren't exaggerating even a tiny pinch about your abilities, were you?"

"Oh, you still ain't seen nothin' yet, Dugan Randall. Just you wait!"

"Well, punching paper is a whole lot different than shooting at another human being. But this is definitely great shooting no matter how you look at it.

"Now let's see how well you remember the bow shooting techniques we practiced last night."

She performed even better with the archery tackle, sticking a tight cluster of six arrows into the center ring on the foam target cube from fifty feet, using the quick instinctive style shooting technique that Dugan showed her, which didn't waste precious time taking careful aim for each shot. He timed her series of shots with his stopwatch, and was surprised enough with the speed of her first six-arrow string that he talked her into repeating the feat, which she promptly did without hesitation. Her second string of arrows were almost identically grouped with her first, but she shaved almost half a second off her earlier time.

Where he really got a shocker, though, was on the sparring mat, rehearsing all of the martial arts moves he had shown her the afternoon before. Jessica seemed to correctly anticipate his every move before he made it, and he very quickly discovered that her speed and agility had somehow become nothing short of remarkable overnight. She took him down three times out of three tries before he fully realized that her brain not only remembered every phase of every move she'd been taught with near perfect precision, but it had actually devised shortcuts and improvements on every one of those moves that allowed her to apply streamlined, more effective techniques of her own.

"Geez," he said, recovering to his feet and catching his breath after his third take-down, "My most advanced Jujitsu student was never able to put me down on the mat even after a year of training, and here you've managed to do it three times after only one lesson! Looks like from now on if I want to up my game maybe I should take lessons from *you*."

"Yeah, I do catch on to things pretty fast, don't I?" she said with a proud smile.

"No wonder you're worth so damned much on the black market!"

She surprised him again with her demonstration of the gun take-away trick that he taught her the day before. He thought her swiftness in the execution of it was quicker than humanly possible. Before he could even blink, she had the imitation pistol out of his firm grip and pointed at his head. He jokingly accused her of using her genie magic on him. He had to admit that he never even saw her hands move.

Now he started thinking really hard about more innovative ways in which he might possibly challenge her.

"Okay," he finally said, "since so much of this stuff seems just a way too easy for you let's see how well you can execute a more intricate task – while wearing a blindfold."

She looked eager for the tougher challenge and enthusiastically rolled the bandana he tossed her into a narrow band that would cover her eyes with its ends like ropes that could be tied behind her head. "Great! What sort of 'more intricate task'?"

"Do you even have to ask?"

She secured the ties on the blindfold with a quick overhand knot behind her head. "No, I don't really. You want to see if I can find a paperclip with this blindfold on and pick the lock of the handcuffs you'll put on my wrists behind my back."

"Once again I'm impressed! But it should be sufficiently challenging and pretty amazing if you're able to do it. What do you think?"

"Let's find out," she said, holding her arms out behind her for him to put the cuffs on her wrists.

He first checked the ends of the blindfold tied behind her head to ensure it would stay in position, and then he put two separate sets of cuffs on her wrists behind her back to restrict her hand movements as much as possible, closed their hasps and slipped the keys to them into his pocket.

"This should be interesting," he said as he pushed the start button on his stopwatch.

Almost immediately a small-sized metal coffee can fell from a shelf on the opposite wall and the assorted fasteners like nails, screws, and the other small miscellaneous odds & ends it contained spilled out onto the floor.

As if guided by the noise of the spill, Jessica made her way to the scattered tiny objects and sat down on the floor with her back to the mess, and leaned backward where her fingers could reach things on the floor. Within seconds she felt what she was looking for, which was a large paperclip, and her fingers started working to straightening it out and bend a small hook at one end.

"You caused that can to fall off the shelf merely with your mind power?" Dugan asked in utter disbelief of what his eyes told him.

"How else would you explain it falling off the shelf all by itself like that, just the way I needed it to do? But don't worry, I'll pick everything up off the floor when I'm done," she replied without appearing to break her concentration.

Seventeen seconds later she had one hasp opened and was already working on another. Before the second hand of Dugan's dial stopwatch had completed three full revolutions, both sets of handcuffs had fallen free from her wrists and she raised herself up from the floor with her hands free to untie the blindfold. She then handed both sets of handcuffs with the bandana to Dugan with a proud grin.

"I can't believe I just watched you move an object with your mind! Pretty sure I've ever seen anything like that before – a fairly heavy object like a coffee can full of odds & ends just pulled right off a shelf with mental power," he mumbled, shaking his head. "Is there anything you cannot actually do?"

"I don't know, but I'm sure there must be."

"Well, I guess the only thing that matters is that you're able to do whatever you will need to do when the time comes. And we still have more training ahead of us. I think we should train with surveillance gear, opening all types of door locks, converting everyday household items into usable weapons, tactical communications, how to defeat thermal imaging and all sorts of alarm systems, how to use night vision optics, clothing quick-change techniques, and so on. Based on what I've seen already you'll master all of these things in record time. Nevertheless, we have a lot of work to do."

Just then Dugan's cell phone started beeping and he reluctantly took the call. Its volume was loud enough that Jessica could hear both sides of the conversation from where she was.

"Is this Dugan?" a female's voice asked.

"Yes. Who's this?"

"I'm Bev Tatum, Bob Morrell's cousin. Remember me? You gave me your phone number three nights ago at Bob's birthday party?"

"Only vaguely - about giving you my phone number I mean. I had a few drinks that night and so I'm a little fuzzy on the details, but yeah, I remember you pretty well."

"Well, I hope you didn't forget that you told me to call you when my schedule freed up. So now I'm free for the next two days and just wondered if you had any dinner plans for tonight? I'm making lasagna. You can ask Bob what he thinks of my lasagna. Have you ever dined on Italian food while soaking in a hot tub?"

"No, ma'am, can't say that I've ever done that, nor ever even been invited for anything quite like that."

"Well, it's a thoroughly pleasant experience I promise. I just happen to have a hot tub and I make killer lasagna, plus I've been saving a vintage bottle of Merlot for the right company. So, what do you say? I live in Fayetteville and I can text you the directions to my place. Do you think you could be here by around seven o'clock?"

He hesitated, looking at Jessica, "I, uh... I just started a new job assignment and it's pretty much 24/7 for a while and not something I can easily step away from right now. But trust me, the thought of soaking in a hot tub with that gorgeous lady I remember from the party, with a glass of wine in my hand and a plate of homemade lasagna appeals to me immensely. Would there be any chance of you being 'free' again later, like maybe in a week from now?"

"Oh, there's always a chance. I guess I can hang onto that bottle of wine for another week."

After the conversation ended Dugan tried to offer an explanation to Jessica, but she acted disinterested.

"Just because I overheard the conversation doesn't make it any of my business," she said, "but you know we can take a little break from our training if you want to call her right back and tell her you'll see her at seven."

"I probably would but I'm afraid she'd find a way to keep me there overnight, maybe for as long as two days or something. We really don't need that kind of distraction right now."

"I guess she must be quite attractive. It's a shame that she's definitely not your type."

"Not my type? So, I guess you're not only able to get inside peoples' heads and know every single thing they think about, but you're also an expert on human relationships and personality compatibility?"

"I suppose that's a fair assertion. I have a special kind of intuition about people."

"And just from hearing a woman's voice over a phone for something probably just over a minute you're able to deduce that she's 'definitely' not my type?"

"It's hard to explain in a way that would make any sense to you, Dugan, and like I said, none of it's my business. But I can promise you that Beverly Tatum is not someone you'd really want to get too involved with. But you could call her back right now and let her know you'll see her tonight if you want to find that out for yourself."

Dugan paused. He seemed to be contemplating Jessica's suggestion. She knew that part of him really wanted to go experience everything that Bev had planned, but his better judgment ultimately won out.

"You know that I'm not going to see her tonight, don't you?" he finally said. "I'll bet you knew that even before I did."

CHAPTER 9

Dugan started pushing Jessica harder in her training. He was now realizing that she could do a lot more than he previously expected of her and so he started pushing her to do more.

"Come on, Jessie! You showed me your absolutely unbelievable speed earlier. That was impressive, but now I need for you to hit harder – a *lot* harder! Pretend you want to put the hurts on that bag. Throw some force behind those punches!"

"I'm not used to being called 'Jessie'."

"Perfect! If that annoys you then perfect. Maybe it'll get you to hit the bag with a bit of saucy irritation. Keep in mind that many of the thugs you could be up against will weigh twice as much as you do. You know it'll take quite a blow to make any difference with some of them."

"I didn't mean that being called Jessie annoys me. I'm just not used to that nickname, that's all. Lately I've been telling people my name is Janice just to avoid coming up on the radar wherever I happened to be. I got kind of used to being Janice."

"I'll call you by whatever name you prefer."

"My real name is Jessica and I've been Janice for a while, but if you want to call me Jessie, that's fine with me, too."

When she started concentrating on the force of her punches, she started hitting the punching bag with increasingly impressive impact. She was beginning to demonstrate remarkable force combined with speed in her punches. It was a good demonstration of mind over matter, despite her light frame and petite stature.

"Now that's what I'm looking for!" he bellowed with excitement. "Your brain is doing what it does best, giving you seemingly supernatural ability. You're unstoppable now."

"Then now we must be ready for Florida," she said wishfully.

"Not exactly," he corrected her, "If you're reading my mind then you know we still have a lot of work to do before we go."

She knew that he was right. They still had to plan the details of their operation, make decisions about which communications methods they'd be using, rehearse every step of the mission, make travel plans and work out all the logistics of everything.

"You'll need video of me all tied up to show those human traffickers that you actually have in your possession what they want," she said.

"That thought did cross my mind."

"I know. Where do you think I got the idea? You just didn't want to say it."

"I wasn't entirely sure how to propose something like that. I mean, tying young girls up and videotaping them isn't exactly one of my hobbies, you know?"

"I know that, Dugan. You don't have to tell me. So, we'll need a video cam."

"My digital camera shoots decent video, and I'm thinking using duct tape on your wrists and ankles just like we did for your training. I think duct tape looks more fittingly realistic for this kind of scenario than either rope or handcuffs."

"Agreed. Shall we get the unpleasant task over with right now?"

Even though he couldn't read her mind like she could his, he could tell she didn't enjoy being tied up at all. It was probably the combination of the cold duct tape wrapped tightly and painfully digging into her skin along with the sense of being restrained. It wasn't fear she showed – she completely trusted him, but it looked more like genuine discomfort. He decided not to tape over her mouth, though, because he didn't want to block out any part of her face from the image and the added discomfort of doing that wasn't really necessary in his view. Besides, her identity would be more verifiable – at least theoretically - with a sample of her voice in the audio, if she were to speak a few words in the video.

In any case, this brief little video shoot wasn't done against her will at all, and that was the important thing. And he also felt fairly certain that if he *were* to leave her alone all tied up it wouldn't take her very long to free herself, now that she'd had the training that he had given her.

After their convincing video was recorded and the sticky duct tape was all removed, Jessica talked Dugan into cutting her hair shorter, and they died her hair dark brown to alter her appearance as much as possible. He hated changing her beautiful flowing auburn hair, but after the changes he discovered that she still looked stunning to him. It actually made her look just a little older, he thought.

When she suddenly closed her eyes and placed her palms on her forehead, Dugan looked at her with concern. "What's the matter?" he asked her.

"Those federal men who were here earlier this morning, they've sent two other men to watch you."

From where she and Dugan were inside the barn not close to any windows, she wouldn't have had any opportunities for visual observation. Dugan knew she was remote viewing with her mind. When he instinctively started for the window, she grabbed him by a shirt sleeve to restrain him. "Might not be such a great idea to be seen suspiciously straining to look out the window," she said. He paused to consider it and then heeded her warning.

"Are they coming to knock on the door?"

"No. They're setting up a surveillance position maybe five hundred feet away, just uphill from the end of your driveway where they've got a view of your Jeep and of the front door of the barn."

"That would be just a few yards past my uncle's property line. Can you determine whether or not they've got listening capabilities, such as with a bionic ear device?"

"I don't believe they do," she said. "I'm sensing visual monitoring only. They're using binoculars for sure. They're setting up a type of hunting blind to camouflage their presence."

"Well, now based on this we can be sure that even if they did before, those agents who visited us this morning no longer have one hundred percent confidence that I was truthful with them earlier. All right then, so now we know we can count on the fact that my actions will be under close scrutiny from now on. This will be just a precautionary measure for them, I think. They're just covering their tracks as professionals."

"That's what my sense is telling me, too," she said. "They're still inclined to believe what you told them earlier, but they've got people watching your place just in case they're wrong."

He paused to contemplate the situation. This was definitely critical information to know under the circumstances. He also needed verification that what she was sensing was accurate, and she recognized this and understood it. She reminded him that the surveillance team's field of view was presently limited just to the front of the barn and the immediate parking area in front, knowing that he would want to quietly exit the building from a door on the opposite side completely hidden from their view and then circle back around where he wouldn't be seen but where he could observe their position. He took a pair of binoculars and a handgun with him.

After he had returned about fifteen minutes later he seemed more confident in his knowledge of the situation.

"Here's what we'll do," he said, after considering their options. "Past the edge of my uncle's property completely hidden from these guys' visibility at the moment and beyond that small crick that winds around in a crescent arc there's a dirt road that doesn't get much traffic. It's just a Forest Service fire break road. About three-quarters of a mile up that road following it to the left it branches off in a Y.

"They'll see me going out my front door *alone* and driving away in my Jeep. But they'll never see you as you exit the same back door that I used just now. If they try to follow me I'll lose them, but they probably won't because they're keeping their eyes on the barn thinking you could still be in here.

"I'll meet you at the Y in that dirt road in say, an hour from now. That should give me enough time to pay a visit to a friend of mine, Derek, and trade vehicles with him. He's been wanting my Jeep since I first bought it and he'll trade me his Ford pickup with a Palomino camper on it straight across for the Wrangler. He's offered me that deal before. He doesn't really like to travel and he hardly ever goes camping anymore, so it'd be a good trade for him. Chances are he'll be home because he's retired and he spends most of his time in his woodshop. He lives about five or six miles away from here. You'll have the trees to hide among if any vehicle besides either my Jeep (if for whatever reason the trade doesn't happen today), or that truck and camper come up that road. Nobody will be looking for you or me in that rig. We won't be coming back to the barn after this, at least not for a while - until things settle down anyway, so you'll want to pack accordingly."

He pulled a large hard-shell acoustic guitar case out of his closet and laid it on the bed, then opened it to check the contents and to add a few extra things. Neatly packed inside were a pair of rubber coated 10x50 binoculars, a night vision scope, two handguns with holsters, a scoped AR-15 rifle, several boxes of ammunition and extra magazines, a stainless steel thermos, a compact hiker's sleeping bag, a small police scanner, a pair of compact GMRS two-way radios, a disassembled take-down recurve bow and eight hunting arrows, a lightweight hatchet, shaving kit, first-aid kit, hunting knife with a sheath, a Leatherman Wave multi-tool, a Ziploc bag filled with twenty-dollar bills, a thin package of latex gloves, bag of energy bars, pair of sunglasses, an olive drab hand towel and a few items of spare clothing including a ski mask, plus miscellaneous other small survival tools and gear. He added his digital camera to the rest of the kit that had the video they'd made.

"When I noticed that case in the back of the closet this morning," Jessica remarked, "I just knew you didn't really keep a guitar in there. Do you even know how to play a guitar?"

"Nope, I've never even touched a guitar in my entire life. But this makes a great emergency bug-out kit. Inconspicuous, you know? I'll leave the barn carrying this and those guys watching me will just figure I'm off to a jam session somewhere."

Before leaving the barn she gave Dugan an unexpected hug and begged him to be careful. He was noticeably caught off guard by this, but he promised her he would be careful and he got her to promise him that she would be, too. He loaded the cylinder of the 357 snub-nosed revolver and handed it to her, saying it was for "just in case emergencies". She took it and put it in her bag.

"Suddenly I hate myself for bringing all this trouble to your door step," she said genuinely. "I guess in hindsight I should have thought everything through more carefully. Nothing good ever comes to the people around me."

"Nonsense. It's been entirely too long since I've had such a good adventure as this!"

"Yeah, well we'll see how enthusiastic you feel about these adventures in a couple of days from now," she said.

"I can appreciate your concern, Jessie, but before you came along I was already being forced to move out of my utopia by the first half of next month, anyway. At least now I have a job, for however long this lasts."

A minute later she exited the door at the other end of the barn as instructed, carrying her shoulder bag containing all of her worldly possessions, and he casually walked out the front door carrying his guitar case and then climbed into his Jeep and drove away.

CHAPTER 10

The two of them reunited at the Y in the dirt road an hour and twenty minutes later. He arrived in the pickup with the camper.
"Sorry I didn't get here a little sooner like I said I would," he said. "The deal took a little longer to finalize than I anticipated. I'll still have to get this thing registered in my name later, anyway. Hope you weren't getting worried yet."
"I wasn't worried. That's one advantage of being cursed with having been born with my level of intuition. I can nearly always clearly sense whenever there is hidden danger or if something is wrong, and I never had that sense here."
"Well, you're on a mission to help people, so even though it's obviously complicated your life in unimaginable ways, I'm not sure I'd characterize your special intuition as a 'curse'. Maybe it's more like a gift."
"You're absolutely right. I should keep reminding myself of that."
"I kept a close watch in the mirrors all the way out here and I didn't see anyone following me," Dugan said.
She looked the new vehicle over approvingly. "This truck/camper setup is really impressive."
"It sure is. It's a 2010 Ford F250 Super Duty long box with low mileage and a 2014 Palomino SS-1500 camper. This is exactly what we need for the traveling we'll have to do."
"So, where do we go from here?"
"Well before we do much of anything else I think we should go into town and get a couple disposable burner phones for untraceable communications. After that maybe some lunch, if you're as hungry as I am."

"You know I'm almost always hungry," she said.

"Gotta fuel the engine for all that brain power, right?"

She grinned, "You know perfectly well that there could be no other possible explanation."

Less than forty-five minutes later Dugan was putting one of the new phones he'd bought to use.

"Nick?" he said when his call was answered, "Hey, this is Dugan. You think you could set me up a meeting with that document forger you recommended a while back, that same guy you've done business with on past jobs? I think he's known as the 'Identity Maker'. I'm on a job right now that's going to need driver's licenses, social security numbers, other documents and maybe weapons carry permits for two people."

After purchasing some groceries and filling up the dual fuel tanks in the truck, Dugan and Jessica were on the road heading south on I-95 S on the first leg of their 120-mile trip to Myrtle Beach, South Carolina. Their meeting with the forger was arranged just as requested by Dugan's friend and they were to meet the man at a diner in Myrtle Beach for an interview.

But the drive down into South Carolina gave Dugan and Jessica time to just talk. It was a little break from the pressures and preoccupation with all the planning and training when they could simply engage in meaningful dialogue. It was an enlightening journey.

"So, how old were you when you first realized you had all of this amazing brain power?" Dugan's question blended with the casual flow of small talk, but she knew he was genuinely curious.

"I was three years old," she recounted an event with perfect clarity, "I remember my dad and a couple of his buddies were in our basement playing pool. Dad brought that pool table home from work one day after his company bought a newer one and wanted to get rid of their old one. So he set that table up in our basement and he would invite some of his friends over occasionally to play on it.

"Anyway, I remember watching one of their games from where I was sitting halfway up the basement stairs, and whenever one of them would take a shot I would put my mental concentration on it in order to influence the outcome. That was when I discovered that I actually had mental influence over the physical world around me without ever lifting a finger, just by mentally concentrating on it. I know now that what I was doing that night wasn't really fair to the players who never had a clue about it, but at three years old I hadn't actually considered the fairness of any of it."

"When did your parents first learn about your extraordinary mental capabilities?"

"Well, my mom died when I was born, so I never knew her. She died from complications in the hospital following my birth."

"I'm sorry. I didn't mean to…"

"No need for apologies. It is what it is. Over the years I've come to terms with it, and now I can accept that I had no control over what happened to my mom, but I don't really know much about her anyway other than just what my dad used to tell me."

"What about your dad? When did he discover what you can do?"

"I was talking clearly and using fairly sophisticated sentence structure and vocabulary before my fourth birthday, and also reading quite a lot by then, so I was still only three years old when my dad noticed that something was a bit different about me. Pretty soon he started taking me to see psychologists and cognitive scientists as I said before, to learn more about what I was able to do, not even considering at that time how it would quickly draw attention to us and eventually bring danger into our lives."

"Looks like it sure has made your life more challenging all right," Dugan observed. "I can't even imagine it."

"What about you, Dugan? I've told you my story. What's *your* story?"

"I thought you already knew everything about me," he said.

"I know quite a bit about you, this is true, but not everything. What are your parents like?"

He paused before answering, "Well, I guess we're a pretty close family, by most standards. I'm an only child. I don't get to see my parents now nearly as often as I used to, or definitely not as often as I'd like to after my dad's job forced him to relocate to Texas. So, they sold their place in North Carolina, which was not too far from my uncle's place actually, and moved to Texas two years ago. I went down there to visit them last spring."

"What does he do for a living, your dad?"

"He's the Editor-in-Chief of *Paranormal & Phenomena Magazine*. He's been with them for at least twenty-two years, so when they announced they were moving their headquarters to Dallas, he and my mom decided to go along, too."

"Must be fascinating working for a magazine oriented around that kind of subject matter," Jessica said.

"Dad literally *loves* his job, I think possibly more than he loves anything else in this whole world. Well, besides Mom, that is. Good thing he doesn't know you exist, though. He wouldn't be able to live with himself until the magazine ran a piece on you."

"You'll just have to keep me hidden away then, safe and secure as your best-kept secret," she said playfully.

He took his eyes off the road for an instant to make eye contact with her. "Naturally," he said, "for national security reasons, of course."

CHAPTER 11

Much of the wall space of the "war room" was covered with maps and charts, and a roll-out projector screen was set up for viewing at one end with the projector atop a center table.

The DHS' Under Secretary of the Office of Intelligence and Analysis, Jason Connors, was presenting the briefing to the small handful of officials in attendance, among them happened to be the Deputy Director of the FBI. Everyone in the room wore a security photo-ID badge clipped to his shirt pocket.

"Good afternoon, gentlemen. I recognize most of your faces but not all. We've got three separate government agencies represented here today. Anyway, I'm Jason Connors from Homeland's Intel & Analysis for those who don't know me. Today's briefing should take no more than about twenty minutes. I understand you've all been briefed on the mission to secure the Prodigy. What I've been tasked with this afternoon is to provide you with some pertinent updates to the situation."

He pressed a button on the projector and four different photo images of one man appeared on the projector screen. Connors pointed to the screen with a yardstick.

"This man's name is Dugan Randall, and his residence on a small farm outside of Fayetteville, North Caroline, was the last known location of the Prodigy, sometime yesterday. Our field agents who interviewed him this morning have reported that he claims to have given our subject a ride to the Greyhound bus station in the city of Fayetteville yesterday afternoon. Our analysts have been studying all bus routes out of that station and I've been informed that there are currently -

or will be very soon - field agents on the ground gathering Intel at every one of the destinations on those routes."

"Who exactly is Dugan Randall and what's his relationship to the Prodigy, or what was the reason she ended up at his place?" FBI's Deputy Director Roger Hendricks wanted to know.

"The only information we have suggests that she most likely sought him out as a body guard. Randall is a twenty-nine year old security guard and martial arts instructor with a military background who currently happens to be unemployed. But his resume is impressive."

"How and where did she see his resume? Where did she learn about this guy?"

"She supposedly did an on-line search and his name came up somewhere, according to *him*, anyway."

Hendricks looked skeptical. "Can we be certain that he hasn't had any contact with the Prodigy since yesterday?"

"No, we can't be one-hundred percent certain of that. We don't have any reason to believe he has, though. But just so you know, Roger, it's one of the surveillance teams from your Bureau's field office in Charlotte that's assigned to keeping eyes on his residence. He was reported leaving that location about three hours ago but in my latest information update right before this meeting he had not yet returned home and his whereabouts at the moment is not known."

Roger Hendricks' facial expression revealed that he was annoyed upon hearing that little bit of information. "My investigating teams will want to learn all about Mr. Dugan Randall," he said. "We'll need to find out exactly where he went after he left his residence. Given that he was her last known contact I think we should be watching him closely. Maybe his story checks out, but then again, maybe there's more to it. Not sure how we'll obtain a warrant to search his premises without having an actual criminal investigation, though. It doesn't sound like he's committed any crimes. At the FBI we're committed to following the legal protocols."

"Thus far he's fully cooperated with our efforts voluntarily, so we didn't anticipate the need for a warrant, and his behavior hasn't raised any red flags with us. But now we're forced to re-think our strategy since we no longer have eyes on him, at least for the moment. But given that this is a matter of high-level national security, certain legal obstacles might be removed. We've got people looking at it and I should have more information to disseminate in the next briefing in twenty-four hours from now."

"Any chance we could get satellite tracking on him?" Hendricks asked.

"We'd have to coordinate that through NSA, and we've been diligent about keeping this whole affair out of their lap up to this point. This sort of thing isn't what they are supposed to get involved in. But we might be re-thinking that strategy now as well."

CHAPTER 12

The Identity Maker seemed to Dugan and Jessica like a paranoid and somewhat eccentric perfectionist. They had no doubts about his experience or his competence and professionalism, even though his look reminded Jessica of an old picture she remembered of Mark Twain from her Fifth Grade history textbook (which she studied at the age of six). His white hair was long and untidy, and he was sporting bushy eyebrows and a bushy mustache.

"I assume Nicholas informed you of my rates?"

"Yeah," Dugan said, "Nick told us you charge five thousand dollars per person needing a new identity, and that you accept only cash and all of it 'up front'."

"Yes, that is correct. But for your money you'll get completely usable new identity profiles with quality documentation and already established good credit, not just a fake picture ID for your wallet. My hacking skills allow me to access data bases and create identities that never existed before, but which appear in the system to have long histories with suitably tailored credentials. And my professional arrangement with a certain real estate tycoon allows me to reserve an apartment unit in almost any major city this side of the Mississippi River, although you'll have to come up with two months' rent deposit if you'll be staying more than a week. But you'll need to show a new residence for your new identities. I've been doing this for a very long time and I've never yet received any customer complaints."

Jessica handed the man a large, thick envelope containing ten thousand dollars in fifty-dollar bills, "That's what we're here for."

He peeked inside the envelope and without taking the time to count the money he tucked it inside his shirt for safe keeping. "So, let's talk about these new identities you wish to assume."

"I'll need to be a chemistry scientist with a medical degree. I'll be posing as a scientist who just developed a breakthrough drug," Dugan pointed out, "and I should probably be a Florida resident, since that's where I'll be registering the pickup and camper I just traded for."

"I'll need to be his wife," Jessica informed the man, "and I would like to be at least twenty-three years old, or preferably a little older like maybe twenty-six or at least old enough to be out of college with maybe a doctorate. Can I be a psychiatrist, or even a psychologist? I've always thought it would be fun to work at a job where I could psycho-analyze people and give them mental counseling."

Dugan laughed, "She doesn't need a special degree or profession to do that, trust me!"

The Identity Maker initially tried talking Jessica out of assuming the identity of a highly specialized professional such as any kind of doctor, noting that with her youthful appearance it could be awfully difficult to be convincing in that role and that could be problematic, especially within certain social circles. But the very instant she started describing numerous details about the University of Washington as if she'd spent years enrolled in medical courses there, and also rattling off a bunch of psychology terminology, he backed off from his initial reservations.

"You've done your homework I see," he acknowledged. "That's good. That's very good – exactly what it takes to make this work successfully. So I might suppose you're fluent in speaking more than one language as well?"

"Presently fluent in four languages altogether," she boasted, "English of course, then Spanish, Arabic, and also Japanese. I can also understand maybe seventy percent of common dialogue in a few others like German and French, but my pronunciation still needs work before I will even attempt speaking any of those."

The man looked amazed, "Seems like an awful lot of stuff to keep track of in that youthful head of yours." Then he looked at Dugan, "How about you? Are you as prepared to act your part as she seems to be for hers?"

Dugan shook his head, "I'll definitely need some study time before I'll fit into my role. But hey, I've got her to help me with that, right?"

The man insisted that they ride in the back of his old 1970's van wearing blindfolds from the parking lot of the diner where they met to his place of operations, which was in an abandoned warehouse, in order to maintain the secrecy of its location. They both cooperated willingly, and it wasn't a very long drive, anyway.

Much of the facility was noticeably dark and dusty inside, Dugan and Jessica noticed upon removing their blindfolds when the Identity Maker said it was okay to do so. But they also noticed that he had some fairly sophisticated equipment set up in there, including three different desktop computers and some expensive-looking printing equipment, as well as a small photography studio with special lighting and background props. A professional-model Leica camera mounted on a tripod faced the portable backboard behind a comfortable looking chair, which was obviously used for creating the photo IDs.

This was where the Identity Maker did his magic, and for the next four or five hours the three of them worked together to create two new identities – identities that could hold up under the closest scrutiny, the man assured them.

Dugan became Dr. Felix McAllister, and Jessica became Dr. Melissa McAllister, and wife of Felix. Her new birth certificate and Florida driver's license showed her to be twenty-six years old.

The Identity Maker advised them to address each other by their new names from now on, even privately, in order to get into the habit of doing so. "You've literally got to *become* your new identities. Your new lives must completely replace your old lives for this to work," he told them. "This also means that if you're going to present yourselves to the world as a married couple, you'd better both be seen in public wearing wedding rings."

They would never know his real name or even any alias for him besides his nickname, the Identity Maker.

The bill of sale that Dugan's friend Derek had written up for the truck and camper left the "sold to" space blank, per Dugan's request. Dugan promised to call him when he had that much decided upon, so that Derek's records would match his own.

Not a lot of explanation was ever demanded or even wanted by Derek about potentially suspicious situations like this that involved his friend Dugan, but the two of them had been friends for years. Dugan also knew that the Jeep would likely never draw anyone's attention who might be looking for him, because Derek didn't drive much beyond running into town once a week for errands such as making beer runs or buying groceries or fresh sheets of sandpaper for his shop, and he drove his old banged up and rusty 1968 Ford pickup all the time for those purposes. The Jeep, Dugan realized, would just sit parked inside Derek's garage, out of everyone's view except Derek's. And Dugan knew that Derek never watched or listened to any news, so if the authorities started looking for him, Derek would probably be one of the last to ever know about it.

As advised they bought the rings for their fingers – for this mission they selected the least expensive wedding bands they could find just to wear in public, at a jewelry store in Myrtle Beach shortly after parting company with the Identity Maker.

The first order of business once they had rolled into Miami the following day was to scope out their new apartment. It was a small apartment with only one bedroom, but it was furnished with a full-sized refrigerator and a conventional oven with stovetop plus a microwave oven, a large comfortable sofa in the front room, and there was even a queen-size bed frame in the bedroom with a new mattress. They would still need to get some blankets and pillows, bath towels, toilet paper, wash cloths and soap and shampoo for the bathroom, cooking pots and flatware for the kitchen, plus some groceries and a few other odds & ends, but this apartment should serve their needs for the time being.

"It's been a couple years since I've been in Florida, and I've only visited Miami once but I had forgotten about all of these palm trees," Dugan said.

"Yeah it's a lot of palm trees. This isn't exactly my first time in Miami, either. My research brought me here a few months ago. That's how I know what I know about what we'll be doing."

Dugan did not bring his sleeping bag from home, but he agreed to sleep on the sofa during their time in Miami. "Seems a shame that newlyweds should sleep separately, doesn't it?" he joked with a wide grin.

"Nice try, dear husband, but I don't think I'm quite ready for our honeymoon just yet."

After picking up the keys and paying the deposit for the apartment, they visited a local insurance agent and purchased auto insurance in the State of Florida for the Ford pickup. If they were to get stopped by police for any reason, this would be one less possible snag or hassle to deal with. This errand was concluded within about forty-five minutes without wasting too much precious time shopping for the lowest rates.

    Next they paid a visit to the local county tax collector's office to get the truck registered in Florida, to Dr. Felix McAllister to match the new insurance papers. This task consumed almost an hour and a half simply because there was a bit of a line to wait in, but it felt good to finally get it done. These were two more things they could check off their list of details that if neglected could have potentially linked them to their former identities.

    Next Dugan looked up information on his newly acquired Motorola pre-paid phone about the closest rifle range open to the public. Jessica (now Melissa) still needed training in how to shoot a rifle, he decided.

    And there were other skills she would also need to be proficient in, like being able to drive. She had never been issued a driver's license before their meeting with the Identity Maker, although she knew the fundamentals of how to drive just from watching others do it. Her brain could pick up details about such things without anyone else paying any attention to what she was doing. But she would still need some hands-on experience.

    "I can show you the basics of how to drive and you're definitely the fastest learner I've ever met, but do you think you could manage driving this truck and camper all the way out to the shooting range, just to get in some driving practice?"

    She nodded confidently, "I've been paying attention to every part of your driving. As you drove you were giving me driving lessons without even knowing it."

And she did impress him with how well she maneuvered the clumsy pickup and camper, through the heavy city traffic as well as out on the highway.

Dugan initially suspected they were being followed when he saw the same vehicle in his side mirror, a gray Toyota Sequoia that he thought he'd seen traveling behind them a little earlier. He didn't mention it right away because he wanted to see if Jessica's supernatural radar would detect it, plus she'd be reading his thoughts about it anyway. When she seemed totally unconcerned he decided to just dismiss it as well. He had probably been just overly paranoid, he figured.

The shooting range was an outdoor range with several target lanes for rifles stretching out to 300 yards. There was a canopy over the shooting benches to provide shade as well as for keeping shooters dry on rainy days, and the shade it provided was a very good thing on a hot sunny Florida day like today. This was also a weekday, so the range wasn't overly crowded – they had one of the rifle lanes all to themselves.

This wasn't the first occasion when Jessica's training put the two of them into a situation involving direct physical contact (he had physically guided her arms, hands, knees, and feet during some of her self-defense moves while coaching her with that, and now he was helping her position the butt of the rifle firmly against her shoulder and her cheek to the stock to find the proper face-to-scope eye relief distance, and also positioning her elbows on the bench for a rigid support), but this was the first time he had a conscious awareness of the closeness.

He liked the way this closeness was making him feel but he wasn't particularly comfortable with the idea that Jessica would also know how it made him feel. This presented a certain dynamic he wasn't exactly eager to embrace right now. He wouldn't be able to conceal his thoughts from her so he just decided that the best he could do was to quickly shift his mental focus away from the thought altogether.

It became obvious immediately that rifle shooting, he guessed like probably pretty much every other physical activity, was an intuitive activity for Jessica. She was able to achieve bull's eye hits with the AR rifle right off the bat, and repeatedly, even at different distances. The rifle was sighted dead on at one-hundred yards, which meant the 55-grain bullets dropped just under three inches at 200 yards, and eleven inches at 300 yards. Dugan knew this information about the trajectory of the 223 Remington ammunition from memorizing a ballistic chart, but he only had to mention these numbers once to Jessica. She had fired a total of sixty rounds and she never missed.

"Damn!" he said after closely inspecting her targets, "I didn't know I was in the presence of Annie Oakley reincarnated."

He let her drive all the way back to their apartment for more practice. By this time she was handling the truck like she'd been driving for years.

"You never cease to amaze me, Mrs. McAllister, you know that?"

"Of course I know it. And I also know that you have quite a crush on me. You can't hide that kind of thing from me you know. We just might have to do something about that a little later."

"Yeah, we just might have to do something about it. But I'll have to learn how to interpret all of your mixed signals first. I feel like I'm pretty much at a distinct disadvantage when it comes to interpreting your thoughts. But for now we should probably focus our attention on the mission, right?"

"Yeah, you're right, we're still on our mission. Hey, on the way back do you mind if we stop at a book store?"

"Sure, why not? What kind of book are you looking for?"

"I don't know exactly – some sort of text book or something on chemistry. We might look for a reference book on college-level biology, too, while we're at it. Remember, we need to make a chemist and a drug developer out of you for this mission and you're going to have to come across like you know something about that whole area of science if this mission is going to be successful. I need to have some reference tools to work with if I'm going to help you with that."

"At least I can say with confidence that I've never had a more, um… *interesting* teacher in all of my school years."

"*'Interesting'?* I'm not sure if I'm supposed to take that as a compliment, or just a polite roasting."

"I thought you could read my mind."

"I don't always read everyone's mind at all times and besides, people don't always form clear thoughts in their heads."

Dugan turned his attention to his side mirror to check if that gray Toyota he had observed earlier was still somewhere behind them. He felt a slight relief when this time he didn't see it. At least at the moment there was no Toyota behind them within his view.

CHAPTER 13

Brandon Carter phoned Tony Byrnell's office immediately upon hanging up the phone after a lengthy conversation with someone else.

"Tony, just reading this note you set on my desk. How soon can you break away from what you're working on?"

"I'll be right over to your office a.s.a.p., Mr. Carter."

Less than a minute later Tony walked into his boss's office, closed the door behind him and sat down in front of the huge executive desk.

"Your note says you've got a new update to report."

Tony nodded, "Encouraging new development for a change. Our eyes and ears inside Homeland Security gave us some unexpected nuggets. Homeland's people neglected to pursue every single possible lead stemming from a tip dropped right into their lap. They missed one that seemed too unlikely, and our mole got some members of his team on it. That seems to have paid off, because now we know where Jessica Knowles happens to be and we have eyes on her, while Homeland is presently clueless."

"Good work! So, where is she?"

"Miami, Florida."

"What's she doing in Miami?"

"The answer to that we don't yet have. We can only speculate. We do have *some* new information, however. We know that she's changed her appearance. She cut her hair and died it dark brown. And, we also know that she's not traveling alone. She's with a guy. It isn't yet clear to us what their relationship is."

"Do you know anything about the guy?"

"Yes, as a matter of fact we do. Our team has done its homework in that area. The guy's name is Dugan Randall. He's got an extensive 'special skills' background and apparently his specialties are personal security and self-defense training and coaching. At this point it's pure speculation, but it seems pretty likely that she hired him as her bodyguard. He's certainly got the qualifications for that."

"Will he be a problem for us?"

"The team believes he can be neutralized. The right opportunity has to present itself for that where he can be dealt with without endangering her, but eventually it always does. At this point it looks perfectly reasonable to expect to have Miss Knowles in our custody by the weekend."

"Excellent work, Tony! I'll relay this to the lab crew so they can have the test facility geared up and ready. Dr. Ellis insists that the science supporting its capability for monitoring and containing brain waves is sound. Perhaps we'll have the chance to test it out sooner than expected."

CHAPTER 14

"I know about the gray Toyota," Jessica acknowledged just as they were returning to their apartment and she was carefully maneuvering the truck and camper under the unit's car port.

Dugan looked at her and sensed she could read the question in his mind. If she knew about it all along, why didn't she say anything?

"I didn't bring it up earlier," she said, "because I wasn't sure about the threat. Now I know more about the threat, and it's definitely something to be concerned about."

"I think we need to have more open communication between us," Dugan said.

They exited the vehicle and walked toward the apartment. Dugan carried a doubled shopping bag loaded with heavy books – they had stopped at a bookstore on their way home just as they'd talked about doing.

"You're absolutely right," she agreed. "I will try to do better with that going forward."

"So, what is this 'threat' you're talking about?"

As they approached the front door of their apartment and Dugan was fishing his key out of his pocket Jessica stopped. "They've been here," she whispered with a tinge of urgency in her voice. "They've been inside our apartment."

Dugan stopped himself before inserting his key into the door and turned to face her. "Who are 'they'?"

"It's more complicated than even I know completely yet, but I have a pretty strong feeling about who they might be and what they want. I know that they're not from the government this time."

"Are they still inside the apartment?"

"No, they're not in there right now. They were in there something like forty-five minutes ago probably and then they left."

Dugan stared at the door and tried to mentally process this new revelation. Then he surveyed their surroundings. She knew he was looking to see if he would notice anyone presently observing the two of them. He didn't see anything suspicious around them.

"We forgot to get a few other things at the store," he said suddenly. "What do you say we go get that out of the way right now? It will give us a little more time to think about this whole situation."

She agreed, and they got back into the truck and drove out onto the street. Again he wanted her to drive. She knew Miami better than he did. To buy some time for thinking and planning, she took the nearest onramp onto Interstate 95, heading north. She planned to stay on it for three or four miles before exiting and then circling back.

"Okay," he said, "let's assume they've planted some listening devices inside the apartment. We should plan it out so that whenever we're in the apartment they'll hear us saying to each other only what we want them to hear, but for the most part not what we're really saying."

"We can buy a notepad and some pens at a store and jot down our communications that we want to keep private. We'll have to make our audible dialogue sound authentic, though, or else they'll suspect we're on to them."

"Too bad I can't read your mind the way you can read mine. That sure would help a lot."

She paused to think before replying. "I hadn't considered this before, Dugan, I mean...Dr. McAllister, but you know what? I think it's possible that the two of us could actually communicate mentally, without having to speak a single word."

"You could just call me 'Honey' if you can't decide between Dugan and Doctor. I promise I won't mind. So you think I can do mental telepathy, same as you?"

"How about 'Felix', since that's your new first name? But yes, I do think you're capable of communicating using mental telepathy. At least I believe you can *learn* how to do it. You can learn how to use your brain in much the same way I use mine. That's what I think separates some people from others. Some have discovered how to use what God gave them, while others haven't yet made that discovery."

"You'll help me make the 'discovery', *Melissa?*"

"Sure thing, Felix, why not?" Calling him Felix seemed almost weird to her now after having known him as Dugan for most of a week already. She knew it was exactly the same for him calling her Melissa.

Dugan glanced at the passenger's side mirror and once again spotted the same gray Toyota Sequoia he'd seen before, now following behind them three cars back.

"I know they're following us again," Jessica said. "They've been trying to keep themselves unnoticed behind us for at least the last mile or so, even after we made that loop back onto 95."

"So, if you know these guys aren't part of the government's surveillance then just what do you know about who they actually are?"

"I believe they're working for a corporation that wants me for their scientific project - their closely guarded secret project. Not sure exactly what they're planning to do with me once I've fulfilled their purpose – whatever that is, but they'll need me alive and healthy initially.

"You, on the other hand, are perceived as merely being in their way. You are in immediate danger, and that's what scares me the most."

"Naturally I appreciate your concern for my well-being, but you didn't hire me just for teaching you how to drive. My career choices have always involved this kind of danger. It's what I do – what I've always done."

"I know, but this time I'm responsible because I got you involved, and so if anything happens to you…"

"I don't remember you holding a gun to my head forcing me to take the job."

She couldn't think of words to say at that point, but her worrying was obvious by the look on her face. And she knew what Dugan was thinking, that it would be pretty difficult to outrun the Toyota with this pickup and camper, and also that it would be next to impossible to hide this big thing in traffic.

"I'll have to confront them," he said. "We've got no way to shake them off our trail otherwise."

She raised her eyebrows, still staying focused on her driving and on the road ahead, "That would be super risky, Felix. I know that I agreed at the start we'll do things your way and I meant it, but if you let these guys have an open shot at you I'm pretty sure they'll happily take it. I think we can create a diversion to get them off our backs, at least for a while."

"What's your plan?"

"You haven't been able to read their license plate, have you?"

"No," he said disappointingly. "They're too far behind us for me to see it clearly. It doesn't look like a Florida plate, though."

"That vehicle should be licensed in the State of Illinois, if I'm not mistaken. The corporation they work for is headquartered in Chicago."

"Did you just plant an idea into my head?"

"No, I don't put thoughts into other peoples' heads, but we're beginning to share our thoughts now. See how this works? Reading can go both ways when two minds are in one wavelength."

He drew his pre-paid phone from his pocket and pressed the numbers on the keypad, 9-1-1. "Let's see if we can get the law on their butts. That'd take them out of the chase for a little while.

"Yes ma'am," he said to the 9-1-1 dispatcher who answered his call, "we're traveling on Interstate 95, heading south through Miami, and there's this gray Toyota Sequoia with Illinois license plates chasing after us. They're shooting at other cars and shooting at ours, too, with shotguns! Where are the police when you need them? People are going to die real soon if the police don't come and stop these madmen!"

Dugan hung up before the dispatcher could ask him any of the inevitable questions. Then he wiped the phone for fingerprints and tossed it out the window onto the road to avoid any chance of it being traced to them. He didn't know whether his call could actually be traced or not – probably not he guessed, but he didn't want to take any chances.

"I realize it's against the law to report false information on the emergency hotline," he said as if he felt some need to justify his action, "but desperate measures…"

"Call for desperate actions," she completed his sentence for him. "But this really *is* an emergency! I'd feel differently about it if it was just a fun prank, but this danger is real."

It wasn't nearly as long as they'd feared – maybe a minute and a half before a patrol car appeared weaving its way up through the traffic behind them with its lights flashing and its siren blaring, quickly spotting the out-of-state SUV and then trailing behind it until there was a safe spot in the road to pull over. The lawmen couldn't have been far away when they received the call. So in this instance the diversion was a success as far as providing them with a quick escape and buying them a little bit of time.

"We need to change vehicles again," they both said in unison. They looked at each other in surprise. "Are we now mentally connected all of a sudden?" he asked.

"I would say we are."

"This could start getting expensive, you know, switching vehicles about every other day like this."

"I don't think we'll need to continue changing vehicles quite this often," she countered, "but I guess whatever we need to do to keep ourselves off the radar, right? Anyway, we should never have to worry about running out of money."

They took the nearest exit and navigated their way to the Unemployment Appeal office on Coral Way. There they met a few people who appeared eager to take on a side job for some quick cash. Their attention was drawn to a middle-aged couple, and Jessica gave Dugan a thumbs-up to indicate she sensed they were trustworthy.

"What we need," Dugan explained to the man and his wife, "is someone to drive our pickup and camper to Dallas, Texas for us where we'll be picking it up in another two weeks or so. We've got some business to finish up here in Miami, but a friend of ours wants to borrow our camper at least a week before we can make it out that way."

Again he didn't feel at all comfortable telling another lie, but only Jessica would be able to detect it because he sounded so convincing.

"We'll pay you a thousand dollars cash up-front, plus another four hundred for gas and for your bus fare home. The truck has most of a full tank right now. I'll get you the address and directions to where you are to leave the truck parked at your destination.

"Now, you might think it would be easy to scam us since you'll already have all your money before even starting the job. But the two of you look like decent honest people to me – and hopefully safe drivers, and there's also a tracking chip hidden on board that you won't likely be able to find. We'll be able to determine where the truck is at all times, and anyway, you've already given us your home address and contact information, so I'm willing to take the chance."

Dugan and Jessica then walked to the nearest used car dealership, Dugan carrying his guitar case and Jessica toting the bag of books along with her gym bag containing the tens of thousands in cash and her other personal effects, slung over her shoulder.

They also both carried concealed handguns, and they both now had the concealed carry permits for Florida that looked authentic. Jessica kept the little Ruger snub-nosed revolver in her shoulder bag, and Dugan's Glock 17 rested in an inside-the-pants holster, tucked away from view and covered by his loose shirt. They stayed off the busiest streets for the most part, hoping to travel outside the view of those looking for them.

"That was a clever one about the tracking chip," Jessica said.

"It was all I could come up with in the moment. Hopefully they bought it. I'm also hoping they won't be in any danger if our pursuers catch up with that rig and find them in it. You really think we can trust them to accomplish that task for us?"

"Yes, I do think we can trust them. And I don't think they'll be in any real danger from our pursuers because it should be clear enough that they didn't know about the diversion strategy they were lured into. But my senses tell me they're going to drive all the way to Texas undetected. That address you wrote down for them, that's where your parents are, isn't it?"

Dugan nodded, "It's actually the parking lot of the magazine publisher where Dad works. I wrote the name of one of his coworker's on that paper as their contact and the person they are to leave the key with - one of Dad's most trusted buddies named Del Crawford, just so there's no traceable link directly to my parents in case our drivers get intercepted before reaching their destination. I'll call Del tonight or tomorrow sometime just to give him a heads up, and I'll call Dad, too.'

By the time they reached a used car dealership they were both feeling tired from the long walk, and also hungry. It had been hours since they'd had anything to eat. There wasn't going to be a lot of time spent on car shopping and test-driving different vehicles today. The cleanest late-model automobile with the least amount of miles on it for the best price would automatically be chosen, and today it happened to be a navy blue 2008 Chevy Equinox LT with 97,000 miles on its odometer.

The window sticker showed a price of $3,250.00, but ultimately, they paid a total of twenty-eight hundred with their out-the-door final deal, after Dugan pressed the sales guy on how quickly he would be able to get the paperwork processed with that cash offer before they walked off to the next dealer down the boulevard. They were in fact starting to leave the car lot when the salesman ran after them, promising he could get them on the road in their chosen vehicle at *their* price within half an hour.

After buying Subway sandwiches at a drive-through, Dugan and Jessica reserved a room at a modest Miami motel for five days. That would give their apartment eavesdroppers plenty of unproductive "sounds of silence" time, and it would ease up a little pressure for the time being. Dugan - Dr. Felix

McAllister – would be able to hit the books and focus on his studies. And Jessica was eager to help him with that.

    The books they'd acquired were college level chemistry and biology textbooks, except for one which was more specifically a comprehensive study of methamphetamine and phenethylamine-related drugs. Alternatively, they could have visited a public library and gotten Internet access on a desktop or laptop computer for possibly all the information they would need, but they decided the paper books would provide them more freedom and the convenience of being able to comfortably study wherever they happened to be, either out on the road or in this case in the privacy of their motel room.

    They were both comforted by the fact that the motel room had two separate beds. This would make their sleeping arrangement much less awkward than would a room with only one bed, as their apartment had where Dugan felt obligated to sleep on the couch.

    Dugan set his guitar case on the floor close to one of the beds and Jessica set her gym bag and the bag of books on the other. They surveyed their new habitation. The room didn't have much besides the two beds, a small closet, breakfast nook, a bathroom, and also a television set.

    "For what they're charging for this for only five days I was actually expecting something a little bigger and fancier," Dugan said. "Not that I care so much about the room or that we'd need any more than this really. I'm just not used to the prices of things in Miami just yet I guess."

    "Yeah, this isn't exactly the most economical town I've ever visited, that's for sure. Lucky for us it'll only be for a week."

    "At least no one will ever think to look for us here."

CHAPTER 15

Dugan was abruptly awakened by the thick envelope that flopped like a paperback novel being dropped onto his chest that Jessica had tossed over to him. He sat up in his bed and blinked twice to clear his sleepy vision, and then examined the envelope closely, "Payday again already?"

She nodded. "You'll be earning it. We have a lot to do today, so I thought I should wake you up sooner rather than later."

"What time is it?"

"It's time to get started. It's already six a.m."

He climbed out from under the bedsheet and flipped the guitar case open. Without bothering to look inside the envelope he tossed it into the case for safe keeping and snapped it shut.

"We should go for a morning run before we do anything else," he said. "I've been off my routine for close to a week now. I'll be lame and lazy if I don't get back into it pretty soon."

"I suppose we could postpone your academic lessons for maybe a half hour or so if you need to get your morning routine out of the way first."

"You'll run with me, right?"

"Sure," she relented, "but you know (as you like to remind me often) I'm *way* younger than you, and you might have trouble keeping up."

He raised his eyebrows but suddenly considered that she might be right about her being a challenge to keep up with, even if she was only joking. God only knew how many miles she must have walked and for how long before they'd met. If anyone he ever knew looked to be physically fit, she sure did.

And she was looking even more attractive to him than she had before, too. He couldn't help noticing that she was blessed with a near perfect figure, and her facial features were petite and nicely proportioned. Her looks seemed to perfectly match her lively and enchanting personality, and he was beginning to feel himself falling...

No, not that again! He definitely didn't need his mind getting distracted with those kinds of thoughts again right now – not with all that they still had ahead of them to do. Besides, Jessica would know every thought he entertained, so he had to at least *try* to steer his thoughts away from her charms and sex appeal, no matter how luring she might be, intentionally or unintentionally. She already knew he was attracted to her, but there'd be no sense in dwelling on it. He quickly shifted his attention to other things.

They dressed themselves in sweats and then went for a short jog that encircled four long city blocks. A little over thirty minutes later they had returned to their motel room, taking turns showering. After they were both dressed and had eaten a cold breakfast and chased that down with a cup of coffee, it was time to hit the books.

"How about you read a couple pages or maybe a chapter and then I'll quiz you on it," she said. "We can get through these books that way. I know you're a quick learner but we've got a lot of material to cover."

After almost two hours of steady reading and being quizzed about chemistry Dugan announced that he could use a short break to refresh his concentration. "That bit in the labor law about requiring a fifteen minute work break after so many hours on the job makes sense to me now," he joked.

"Oh yes," she said in her sarcastic humor. "We must stay within those legal boundaries straight on down the line. But actually, a break right now *does* sound like a good idea."

She gently closed the textbook and set it on the nightstand between the beds, then glanced around the room like she was searching for something, finally opening the little drawer in the nightstand where she found a small notepad and a stubby pencil. She jotted something down on the notepad, then tore the tiny page from the pad and stuffed it into her pocket out of sight.

"Alright," she said, lying back on her bed and looking up at the ceiling. "Let's try a little experiment. Try lying on your back just like I'm doing, and clear your mind of all distant thoughts. Let me know when your head is clear."

He did as she suggested, laid back on his bed. "What are we doing?"

"You'll see. Let me know when your mind is empty."

"Okay. Now my mind is completely blank. Well, blank except for thinking how unproductive this seems to someone who's being paid five hundred dollars a day. So, now what?"

"Now try to imagine that you're a radio receiver and that the people around you are broadcasting stations. You're going to tune in to their broadcasts."

"Just like that?"

"Yeah, just like that, but you have to really concentrate with a clear head or it just won't work. Concentrate. Tell me, what am I 'broadcasting' right now? I wrote it down on that piece of paper so you'll know without any doubt if you actually do get it right."

He was lying comfortably horizontal on his bed exactly as she requested, motionless on his back, concentrating as hard as he could. She waited patiently for him to see her mental vision in his head and then tell her what he saw. A full minute transpired quietly while he tried to focus his attention.

She was almost ready to give up on it for the time being – thinking about opening the textbook back up to where they left off a moment ago when he blurted it out, "We're birds!" he said. "You and I are eagles flying not too far apart, high up in the sky and looking down on the busy world below us. I can even feel the warm air current we're gliding on, like a steady wind in my face. That's what I think you were imagining just now."

She sat up instantly and looked over at him and he looked at her, noticing the surprised look in her eyes. She pulled the piece of notebook paper from her pocket and handed it over to him.

"Didn't expect you to get it this fast," she told him. "But that's how it works. Not terribly difficult when you're properly tuned in, is it?"

He read what she had written on the paper. "That's just crazy!" he said. "How was I able to do that?"

"I believe anyone can do it if they open their minds up to the possibilities. It's literally; mind over matter (if you don't mind the cliché), accessing and employing your brain's inherent power, and as you saw just now it's a real thing. Most people don't believe it's real - they don't believe they can do it, so consequently they can't."

"Will I be able to read other peoples' minds, or did it only work for me this time because you were helping me with your brain power and you *wanted* to share your thought with me?"

"Naturally, sometimes it works better than other times, but whenever your mind is tuned to others' brain waves, you'll know their thoughts. Once you know how to do it you can never completely unlearn it."

"You and I should be able to totally communicate mentally then, right? No more need for us to sound out words with our mouths or even to write any notes to each other on paper."

"That is basically true, but it takes some practice to achieve the level to where you could rely on it solely as a communication method. In that sense it's no different than applying martial arts successfully, target shooting, or other mind and mind-body coordinated activities, which includes basically everything we do. Tuning into others' brain waves is also a skill that is refined with practice."

"Maybe we should start practicing right now," he mentally said to her without moving his lips.

"I think it's a pretty good idea," she replied, also mentally. *"You'll get used to it. You'll also discover that not all thoughts come across a hundred percent clearly. It's really no different than verbal communication in that sense, but instead of using your ears for hearing, you use a different sense."*

Dugan was encouraged with this newly acquired skill. He would be gaining new insight into the thoughts and motives of the people around him, and it would give him and Jessica both an enormous advantage while pursuing this mission.

Soon it was back to the books studying chemistry and the formulae of drugs.

"I guess I never realized how much math is involved with learning about chemistry," he said. "Math has never been my strongest subject."

"A lot of it is just getting your mind accustomed to the metric system for measurements, since that's what is used in the sciences."

"And I'm probably the only bodyguard in the world whose job requires learning chemistry. Now I feel like I can explain to anyone the difference between mixtures and compounds, or between an acid and a base in such a way that they'll understand it. I personally never gave much thought to any of this stuff before."

"Free on-the-job education that prepares you for possibly higher academic vocations down the road. No worries," she half joked, "you can thank me later when you land a high-paying position with an established pharmaceuticals company."

"We still have to invent a drug, you know. Even though we won't actually have this new drug, I've got to make them believe I do for this to work."

"If they see a complex chemical recipe with lots of words they can't pronounce they'll be inclined to believe," she assured. "We might be able to download a patent application from the Internet maybe at the library, and create our own new formula that looks totally legit. These people are narcotics dealers, pimps, and human traffickers, not so much chemists or pharmacists. Basically, if they can be convinced you're not working with the FBI you'll look credible to them."

"That's a pretty big 'if'."

CHAPTER 16

"I still don't like this plan any more than I did in the beginning," Dugan said finally, "and maybe even less now since I've had more time to contemplate everything. It's just too dangerous, you know? It's crazy! You hired me as your bodyguard mainly, to protect you from danger, not to help you get *into* danger."

"I hired you for this mission more than anything else, but I don't believe there's any other way to save those girls from their life-long enslavement. Anyway, this is my purpose in life right now – shutting down that trafficking ring."

"If anything bad happens to you I'm not sure I could live with myself. Whether good or bad I ultimately agreed to become a part of this insanity, and in so doing I became responsible for your safety. You're not even legally an adult yet."

"Thanks for reminding me again that I'm just a child in your eyes," she quipped with more than a hint of annoyed sarcasm. "Well, I'm committed to do this, either with you or without you."

He rolled his eyes, "Yeah, because you know I won't be able to let you do it alone."

Suddenly she couldn't hide her smile when she heard what she wanted to hear, and suddenly it also felt like a perfect moment to switch the subject. "That patent application sure was a lot of work, but I really do think it looks good – looks totally professional and scientific."

He nodded, "I agree, it does look impressive. For all practical purposes you're the real doctor here. Your authoritative-looking notations and explanations almost have me believing you've actually developed a new drug that would achieve what we say it will. I just hope it's convincing enough to *them*. Pretty much everything hinges on that document. If they don't believe I've invented a viable new drug, then our entire plan crumbles."

"I'm super encouraged by the fact that after only three days of immersing yourself in this stuff you already sound like you've devoted your entire career to developing medicines," she said. "I'm confident that you'll be very convincing when you'll need to be."

"Now I need to learn more about their organization."

She sighed, "Um, where to begin? I honestly don't know exactly how many people make up this criminal enterprise but I can tell you that an FBI report estimated there were between fifty and sixty people on the payroll in 2016, more than fifty percent Floridians of Cuban and Puerto Rican heritage. Their trafficking operations are known on the street as the 'meat auction'. Also, according to the FBI this particular one is the largest international sex trafficking ring based in the United States.

"They also run a faux charity ironically called *Humanity's Advocate*, through which they launder literally tens of millions of dollars in 'dirty' revenues. The head of their organization - their 'Jefe', is most often referred to as *El Tirano* (Spanish for 'The Tyrant'). At least he's known on the streets of Miami as El Tirano and apparently he's content with the nickname, but probably only those in his closest inner circle know his real name - even the FBI isn't a hundred percent sure of his true identity. He's a ruthless business man and that's where he got his nickname. Like I've said before, unbelievable amounts of money change hands in this business. The money is the source of all this man's influence and loyalty. He's able to rely on his people to carry out his wishes because money is a very powerful influencer."

"What can you tell me about their place of business?"

"I'll be able to show you where the building is located, but I don't have any information about the floor plan layout or what kind of security they have inside. They've moved their operations twice since their dealings with the FBI, and they've tightened up their security. I don't have any clues at all about where they keep the 'merchandise', except that I'm pretty sure the girls are not held in the same building or even at the same general location as their main business headquarters."

"That makes sense. But we've got to figure out where they keep those girls one way or another. And we can't count on getting eye witnesses in the swap because it's only logical that the girls will be blindfolded before being moved. Maybe FBI interrogators would be able to somehow extract useful information out of them – they're experts in that area - but we don't dare involve the FBI in this – not with the feds working overtime trying to hunt you down."

The words came out of his mouth, but as soon as they did he realized – and Jessica knew what he was thinking and she also knew that what he was thinking happened to be absolutely right – that ultimately they *would* need to involve the FBI. It would be the only way to finally shut down this crime ring once and for all.

The trick, of course, would be in delivering one or more rescued kidnap victims to the custody of federal agents without drawing attention to themselves. And even if they were successful with that there would be no guarantees that any usable evidence whatsoever could ultimately be obtained as a result. It seemed like a lot being risked for the odds against it actually working.

"If we were to somehow plant a tracking device with them, then maybe we could… No, no good. They would discover it too easily. We can bet they'll sweep everything that passes through their door with a bug detector," Dugan mumbled, thinking aloud. "If they found a device we had planted it would seriously derail all of our efforts."

"Yeah, and probably get one of us or both of us killed."

"Might get *me* killed possibly, but like you said you're worth too much to kill. Another possibility is we could monitor their place of business. I'd be for surveilling their premises and maybe tailing any vehicles that come and go to see where they go, except that I seriously doubt they'd leave it all so easy for us or for anyone else to do that."

"I believe you're right. I thought of the idea, too, but it wouldn't be easily doable in this case. They share a parking garage with at least two neighboring businesses (which they most likely also own), including an adult film studio and also a nightclub that gets a lot of customer traffic. I didn't see any good locations from which to secretly surveil the entrance to that garage when I scouted the whole vicinity about three weeks before I met you. Additionally, there'd be no way from outside the garage to see whose cars belong to whom anyway. There'd just be too many cars to tail, or to keep track of, even if we *had* a safe view of them coming and going."

"Your detective intuition never ceases to amaze me," he said. "So then, now that we've identified all the bad ideas, got any *good* ideas for getting the info we need that you'd like to share with me?"

There was a pause in the dialogue. Jessica seemed to be fresh out of ideas, at least for the moment.

"I think we should go for a drive in the city or a stroll through the park for like maybe an hour just to clear our heads before we spend any more time and energy trying to figure everything out," she suggested, signaling that she had no operational strategy formulated in her mind yet. "Maybe we could stop somewhere and eat some ice cream or frozen yogurt?"

Dugan nodded. He liked that idea. His brain needed a break from memorizing chemistry formulas and from trying to figure out impossible solutions to dangerous problems, at least for a little while, like an hour or maybe two.

Less than a half hour later the Chevy Equinox was parked on Biscayne Boulevard within walking distance of an ice cream parlor. The weather was sunny and hot as one would expect in the Miami area this time of year.

They stepped in front of a visibly tired and scruffy old man who was sitting on the sidewalk with his back rested against a lamp post, holding up a crudely written sign on a sheet of cardboard that said; "Hungry! Please help!"

Jessica stopped in front of him and knelt down to make eye contact with him. She saw the despair in his wearied eyes. She could actually feel the weight of his suffering.

"I will bring you something to eat, Sir,' she promised him. "Can you stay right here for another fifteen or twenty minutes? I will be right back with food and something to drink."

He nodded that he understood. She stood up and turned to Dugan, "We've got to feed this man. He's hungry." Then she started walking up the sidewalk at a lively pace looking for the nearest sandwich shop. Dugan followed closely behind her.

"Lots of people in this world are hungry," Dugan pointed out. "Millions of people in India, Haiti, Ethiopia, Sudan, and in so many other African and other countries are literally starving to death. You can't feed the whole world."

"I realize that," she snapped defensively, "Of course I cannot feed the entire world. Probably lots of things I can't do that I wish I could do, but I *can* feed this man right now."

"Sure, you can buy him a meal. Just by looking at him it's pretty obvious that his problems are much bigger than could be cured with one meal. You'll feed him today, but then what will he do tomorrow, and then the day after that? Begging is a daily ritual for a man like this."

"He's hungry. He's pleading for help, and so as human beings I believe we have a moral responsibility to help him. The Holy Scriptures teaches us this over and over. Let's see, how about Proverbs 21:13 for starters, which says, 'Whoso stoppeth his ears at the cry of the poor, he also shall cry himself, but shall not be heard.'"

"So, you're not just a simple psychic mind reader with superior intelligence and seemingly magical mental powers who can speak four languages fluently and solve complex math equations in your head within seconds, but you're also a Bible scholar to boot?"

"I wouldn't say I'm exactly a 'scholar', but I have read every Old Testament and New Testament book in the King James Bible, and I remember everything that I've read."

"Yes, I am pretty sure you do all right, based on everything else I've seen you do.

"So tell me then, does the Bible say anything at all about staying focused on the mission at hand? The mission we're on is about much more than giving a little temporary comfort to an old man who's basically given up on trying to better his own situation, but about actually saving a number of people from a life of slavery and wicked abuse they've fallen into mostly through no fault of their own. You know we could probably find dozens of homeless people in just this section of Miami alone, and we could easily spend a week or longer feeding all of them, and then after that find a dozen more and…"

"Yeah, yeah, I get your point. Of course I won't be able to feed everybody in the world who's hungry. I know that! But I *can* feed this man today, and so I must. I absolutely must.

Ultimately my 'mission at hand' is helping people who need help, and he needs my help."

"Okay," Dugan relented, "let's go get him something to eat then." He glanced back at the image of the lonely old man huddled on the sidewalk. "He's sure lucky that you came along when you did today."

CHAPTER 17

The time had finally come for the well-planned sting operation, and Dugan was very good at concealing his anxiety. The details had all been sorted out and this moment seemed to be as good a time as any.

He arrived at his destination via a taxicab at precisely 9:00 a.m., carrying a large envelope containing the documents that would help him detail his offer, as well as the digital camera with the video showing Jessica all tied up.

The front of the building didn't impress Dugan as an office headquarters for a thriving crime business. It appeared to be a fairly large brick building, but it had to be seventy or eighty years old easily, and something about the outside made it look neglected, at least in Dugan's eyes. The adjoining nightclub was clearly much newer and far more attractive.

He had decided to wear a business suit with a sport coat and neck tie for the professional image he wanted to project. Also, after much contemplation he finally decided to leave his weapons at home. What needed to be accomplished today shouldn't involve any gun fighting, he reasoned. Besides, if things took a bad turn and he were to end up in a gun fight he knew that he would have a reasonably good chance of disarming whoever might be nearest to him and commandeering their weapons. He had extensive training in such situations and his reflexes were nothing short of lightning fast. Chances were nobody would expect a guy in a suit and tie to have his level of skills.

But right now, he kept his focus on staying relaxed and being convincing in his role playing. Right now, he would play the con man who would be a key player in taking down an evil enterprise, *if* everything went according to the plan – a pretty big "if".

    The building's security system was considerable as was expected. The front door's handle was accompanied by a coded lock box with push buttons. Dugan had to push another larger button and speak into a microphone, identifying himself and stating his business while looking into a security camera before anyone would open the door. And as expected the voice he heard over the system was rude and bossy, and he detected a perfectly understandable tone of suspicion in it.

    "I am Dr. Felix McAllister," Dugan responded, "and I have some things I'm sure will interest your boss. I wish to have a meeting with El Tirano."

    "That depends on what you have."

    "Tell him I have a business proposition for him. I've been years developing a totally new drug that I'm confident will more or less replace methamphetamine on the streets within two or three years. I figured your boss might want to be in on the production and supply end of it early in the game before everyone else is. I also have a valuable prisoner who's too valuable for what I need a test subject for. So I'm willing to make a trade."

    "You could be a cop working for the FBI."

    "Yeah, anything is possible. But I'm definitely not a cop. I'm a drug developer and a pretty good business man and that's why I'm here. You can check my credentials in science and chemistry. I even brought my patent application with me to show your boss the formula for it. I also have video in my camera of my prisoner, who happens to be someone the Department of Homeland Security has been trying to locate but hasn't been able to with all of their resources. Ask El Tirano if he's ever heard the name, Jessica Knowles?"

"You wait right there," the voice demanded, and then the speaker box below the security camera went silent.

Dugan hated the wait. It seemed to last a long time, though in reality it was probably no more than three or four minutes. As he waited, he felt the gentle breeze that had rolled its way up from the Keys in the south, and it made him wish he was out on a boat peacefully drifting on the rolling waves somewhere off the coast, fishing or just relaxing.

This whole strategy that had been meticulously planned for days now seemed even more unrealistic and even more precarious than it did before, and he was finding himself wishing for the first time that he had never accepted Jessica's job offer in the first place. He was struck with a premonition that the task wasn't going to go as planned, or at least wasn't going to be as easy as it could be. He was sensing some kind of evil vibe that occupied the space inside this building.

Then the door finally opened and a man ushered him inside. When he did as he was directed, he was received by two other men who were both bigger than Dugan and made him think of nightclub bouncers due to their robust size and build; one of them relieved Dugan of his digital camera and envelope, then searched his pockets and confiscated his set of keys and his wallet. The other man frisked him carefully from his neck to his ankles searching for weapons. Then the same man who'd frisked him waved an electronic wand over the contours of his body, which Dugan realized was to detect any possible electronic listening devices. Fortunately, he was wearing no devices like that for them to find.

Dugan didn't even consider protesting the treatment at this point, knowing that any resistance to their actions could quickly derail the whole the mission.

Next, they led him down a hallway and into a fairly large room with a large one-way window in one wall behind which viewers could watch whatever went on in this room while keeping themselves hidden from view, a few chairs and what looked like a work table occupying the center of the floor. Dugan recognized this arrangement as an interrogation room, and most likely also a kind of torture chamber. El Tirano was not in the room. The front door man left the room and only the two "bouncers" stayed with their visitor. He could hear the room's only door being latched, and the sound of it added to his already uneasy feeling.

When Dugan noticed one of them gathering steel shackles with cables attached to them from a drawer in the table, presumably for securing Dugan's wrists and ankles, he decided it was time to protest.

"Look, I came here to meet with El Tirano - to offer an opportunity for a lucrative and friendly business relationship. I came in good faith. So where *is* he, and why all this?"

"Shut up and sit your ass in the chair," the nearest one holding the shackles ordered him. "We'll ask the questions."

The man didn't expect or even see the high swift and powerful roundhouse Dugan threw to his throat, planting the sole of his expensive shiny new leather wingtip shoe into the man's esophagus with timber-snapping force and sending him to the floor reflexively holding his throat with both hands a split second after the steel shackles plopped onto the floor, choking with his crushed windpipe and possibly paralyzed from the severe trauma to his carotid arteries and cervical plexus.

The second man positioned roughly ten feet away instinctively pulled his pistol from his small-of-the-back holster and swung it up to align his sights on the moving target, but his reaction time wasn't fast enough to dodge the chair flung at him with enough force to knock him backwards, thoroughly derailing his aim and throwing him off balance.

Before he was able to recover Dugan had him partially restrained in a solid neck hold from behind and was able to force the handgun free from his grip by jamming his wrist against a chair leg with his right hand.

The man struggled and resisted, dragging Dugan from side to side while simultaneously retrieving a switchblade with his unrestrained left hand from a side pocket of his Khakis. The blade was quickly noticed and before the man was able to stab anything with it Dugan raised his rigid arm hold over the man's ears like a wrench and twisted swiftly and forcefully in a clockwise motion until he felt and heard the man's neck snap at the base of his skull.

Dugan let the lifeless body fall free as he retrieved the pistol from the floor. It was an HK P30. He noticed that the grip shape seemed to fit his hand perfectly but he didn't have much time to look the weapon over very carefully because as he was doing this several armed men were entering through the door with their pistols drawn.

"Don't shoot! Nobody shoot!" a commanding voice sounded from just outside the doorway.

Dugan froze but kept his newly appropriated pistol aimed at the others in the room, first at one and then another, but they all holstered their handguns and stopped short of rushing him. Then a short and burly Latino stepped into the room. Presumably he was the one who'd given the order not to shoot, and he was clearly in charge.

"You took down two of my men," he said calmly though accusingly.

"I wasn't all that eager to be shackled to a chair and tortured by your men. Maybe I won't make it out of this building alive but I'd rather go down fighting than shackled to a chair," Dugan was now aiming his pistol at the big boss.

El Tirano looked at the two men on the floor – one already dead and the other obviously close to death in his final stages of suffocation with a dramatically swollen neck and throat and a face turned blue, and then he looked at Dugan,

"That is something I respect. And you have cojones coming here alone and unarmed. But how does a chemist and a business man come to possess this kind of fighting skill?"

"From a lot of years studying chemistry while also studying martial arts just to stay fit."

"I am impressed, Dr. McAllister. ¡Muy impresionante! Please join me in my office where the two of us will now discuss business." He nodded to his men to clear away and let Dugan alone. Dugan tucked the pistol under his belt behind him to keep it handy just in case more trouble arose. Then he looked at the two men on the floor, "What's going to happen with those two?"

"Weighted down and tossed over the edge of a boat five miles off shore. My guys get paid well for taking out the trash."

Dugan felt his sweaty shirt sticking to his skin and he was suddenly very conscious of the fact that his nerves were in a tight bundle, even still. Fortunately, he was very good at not letting his anxiety show. He untangled his necktie as he followed the crime boss out of the interrogation room and down the hallway to his office.

The full gravity of having just killed two people hadn't completely sunk in yet, but he did have a conscious awareness of having done it and of the fact that he would have to sort it all out and find the orientation with his own moral compass later on when he wasn't so preoccupied with just keeping himself alive. The events in this room had transpired quickly, too quickly to sort it all out as they were happening.

He remembered what Jessica had told him about imagining himself being a radio receiver and the people around him broadcasting stations whereby he would be able to tune into and actually intercept their thoughts. He focused on tuning into El Tirano's thoughts, and he was able to decipher that the crime boss was surprisingly enthusiastic about striking up a business relationship with this drug developer who couldn't be suppressed by two nightclub bouncers.

As might be expected it was a spacious and plush office. El Tirano closed the door behind them and then gestured for Dugan to take a seat in a large leather-covered chair in front of his massive oak executive desk as he headed for a liquor cabinet. He opened the cabinet door and retrieved two glasses and a bottle of Crown Royal, and filled both before handing one to Dugan. Dugan didn't even consider refusing it, even though he had never been much of a drinker of hard liquor. He reasoned to himself that a few sips of whiskey might actually help him loosen up a little. He and El Tirano were the only two in the office.

El Tirano's look was consistent with the image he evidently cherished projecting. His rugged and leathery coffee-colored face bore a noticeable scar that angled from below his left eye down to his jaw, ending just below his ear. He wore a bright multi-colored Hawaiian style short-sleeved button-down shirt with an oversized collar, and his biceps were almost football-sized boulders bulging up under the hairy tight skin of his short thick arms. Both of his arms sported tattoos, and he appeared to be in his late thirties or early forties. Dugan marveled that his speech suggested a formal education that seemed to betray his tough appearance.

Dugan's attention was drawn to a small table next to the chair he sat in upon which his large envelope, digital camera, set of keys, and wallet rested.

"We checked your driver's license and other cards in your wallet, Dr. McAllister. At least those say you are who you say you are. I am curious to hear more about this business proposal you mentioned."

Dugan picked up the envelope from the table beside him and set it in front of El Tirano on his desk. "For the last six years I've been developing this new drug. I've already applied for the patent and this is a copy of my application, which includes the complete formula. I've done a fair amount of laboratory testing with rats and monkeys, but as yet have not tested it in live human beings.

"The reasons I believe it will soon replace methamphetamines and other popular drugs on the street should be compelling. Not only will it provide the same kind of strong central nervous system stimulation that meth provides and can also be used in treatment for certain undesirable medical conditions just as methamphetamines can, but because it's not a racemic free base chemical it won't have some of the nasty side effects such as potentially inducing psychosis, or causing seizures, or the breakdown of skeletal or muscle tissues often associated with the chronic use of meth. For you the bottom line is that your customers will stay healthier and live longer, and young beautiful ladies will stay young and beautiful much longer."

El Tirano looked at Dugan with suspicion, "What would you know about my 'customers'? Where does all of this information you seem to have about me come from?"

"I've done my homework. I've spent a fair amount of time in the streets of Miami and I've asked a lot of people a lot of questions. I'm an inventor and a business man, and I aim to learn what I need to know to build an empire," Dugan took a quick drink and set his glass down, looking El Tirano straight in the eye, "I just figured you'd be interested in a business relationship that could benefit us both. Together we could control the production, licensing if we can get FDA approval (and I believe we can), and the sale and distribution of this product through all channels, both legal and otherwise."

El Tirano picked up the envelope and removed the papers and glanced over the first two pages. He looked up at Dugan.

"And you're here because you want me to bankroll the operations."

Dugan nodded, "That's partly true. I have a small laboratory up in Gainesville, but a full production facility for synthesizing drugs - ideally located in Miami for logistical convenience - would ultimately be needed. I can plan on maybe throwing a hundred seventy-five thousand at it just to get the ball rolling but to set up the infrastructure needed for production will require at least another half million over that."

"My men said you mentioned somebody's name."

"Yes, a young lady who says her name is Jessica Knowles. My inquiries that eventually led me to your organization also lured this attractive young lady to the apartment I'm renting here in your beautiful city. So she tells me this crazy-ass story about how she wants to get revenge on you for destroying her life. I couldn't get her to share too many details with me but she seems pretty convinced that you've been trying to find her. She had big plans of getting to you first. She says she's been on the lam for over a year staying safely outside your reach, plotting her revenge the whole time.

"So anyway, when I found out she just wanted to use me to get to you, I decided to turn the tables on her. Currently my people have her safely secured where she won't be escaping from our custody," Dugan reached for the digital camera and set it on the big boss's desk, "I brought video evidence that we have her in custody. I thought you might possibly entertain a trade."

El Tirano glanced down at the camera resting on his desk while he took a slow sip of whiskey, clearly processing the information. "Why should I care whatever happens to some delusional teenage street girl who claims to have some beef with me? There's definitely no shortage of young harlots in this city who'll make those same claims," he chuckled.

Dugan pretended to look disappointed. "Yeah, well, I didn't thoroughly believe her story anyway. No worries. We can still use her for our drug testing. She looks healthy enough for what we'll need. And now it looks like she's disposable, which is also what we need."

"Just curious, what kind of trade were you thinking about?"

"So, the extensive testing that needs to be conducted with this new drug chemical is ideally done with healthy, youthful human beings. It would be especially useful to know the drug's effects on people in the age group of say, thirteen to nineteen years old. Three test subjects, either girls or boys in this age group would be very useful, and it doesn't particularly matter whether or not they've participated in prostitution activities, as long as they're healthy. They have to be healthy, and this means free of sexually transmitted diseases, and we wouldn't be able to use any drug addicts – their bodies have to be clean of drugs."

"You are telling me that you will trade Jessica Knowles for three other disease-free, drug-free teenagers, for the purpose of using them as lab rats in your drug experiments?"

"Three are much better than one for this purpose, yes."

"You don't ask for any cash?"

"If we end up in a business arrangement to manufacture and distribute this new drug then I'll be asking you for some financial backing, but I'm not seeking money with this particular trade. Right now, I just need the lab rats."

CHAPTER 18

Jessica experienced a high level of anxiety that was rather uncharacteristic of her while Dugan negotiated with the crime boss. As much as she wished she could, she simply couldn't be with him as he met with El Tirano, not even remotely. And she couldn't shake her sense of responsibility - her sense of *guilt* - for putting him in that very dangerous situation. Suddenly she couldn't stop thinking about his skepticism of the whole plan before this morning, and his repeated objections.

Her psychic senses would often predict the outcomes of events but she didn't always receive a perfectly clear vision into the future. Even with all of her extraordinary mental power she felt powerless in this present situation. This time it seemed like no matter how hard she concentrated or tried to clear her mind, nothing conclusive would enter her brain.

The degree of relief she felt when Dugan finally returned safely to the motel room was beyond words. She gave him an emotional and long-lasting hug the kind of which he'd never received from anyone before. If he had had any doubts about how she felt about him previously, those were totally erased now.

"The big boss went for the deal. I'm probably a better con man than I am a body guard I hate to say. Ironically, I have always despised con men.

"Anyway, the road was a little bumpy at first, but then…" Dugan's enthusiastic expression suddenly changed to more serious, "I killed two men. It couldn't be avoided."

She looked stunned. "I am so, *so* sorry. Have you ever had to, um, I mean in your line of work ever kill anyone before?"

"I've found myself in plenty situations where I easily could have been forced to do it. I am definitely trained in all sorts of lethal techniques but until today I've never actually taken human life."

"I don't know what to say except that I am very sorry I coerced you into that predicament."

"I wouldn't exactly say I was 'coerced'."

"Yes, you were. If I hadn't dragged you kicking and screaming into this whole tangled plot… I think it's pretty obvious this time how my pushy stubbornness could have easily gotten you killed!"

"Yeah, well, as it turns out I'm not so easy to kill."

"But if everything had gone wrong and you had been killed, your blood would've been on my hands."

"You're actually starting to sound like a broken record worrying about me and blaming yourself for my circumstances all the time, you know that? We both know I'd most likely still be unemployed if I hadn't taken your job offer, and I don't remember you ever promising me adventures on Sesame Street, anyway. Just try not to lose sight of what we're doing because what we're doing should free a lot of young people from a life of brutal slavery – we'll be rescuing them from the shackles of these truly wicked people. No, I don't expect to ever feel much remorse at all for killing those two men."

"Okay then. So where do we go from here now?"

"The clock is ticking. I agreed to meet El Tirano with you in my custody at five pm in a wrecking yard on the northern outskirts of Miami, which he said hasn't been in operation for over a year. His guys will cut the lock and open the gate for us. I convinced him that I could have my people transport you from Gainesville where you're being held captive, which is almost three hundred and fifty miles away, and have you available to trade by five o'clock this afternoon. He agreed to bring three of his youngest and healthiest slaves to trade for you."

"Nice! And what will I be expected to wear to this festive slave exchanging party? What do high-priced slaves wear these days?"

"Good one! But seriously, neither you nor I will be attending this meeting. He told me to look for his yellow van and I told him I will arrive in a white van – a white van that I don't even have! Instead, however, I expect that a few FBI agents would rather take my place. They could show up in a white van with tinted glass that hides their faces. El Tirano and whoever goes with him ought to have some fun explaining to the feds why they're transporting several young ladies all tied up in the back of their van."

"Do you think there's any chance he'll smell a trap and just not show up with the merchandise?"

"Anything's possible, but I had a sense this morning that he fully expects the trade to happen. He was quick to point out how fruitful business relationships are based heavily on trust in this industry and that double-crossers never live very long. But he must've felt somewhat assured that I'm not working for law enforcement the way I showed up with my convincing identification, plus that video tape of you in my possession. Not too likely that the FBI would have any video of you all tied up like that."

"Maybe he doesn't necessarily think this is another FBI sting, but he *could* suspect that you and I are working together against him."

"Like I said, anything is possible. But what are the odds of that happening - you and I working together? I'm not too worried about him making that connection."

"Yeah, that would just be crazy; you and I working together. What are you going to say to the FBI when you tip them off about the meeting?"

"I guess I'll have to wing it – I'll be the anonymous tipster. The FBI has an office in Homestead, almost thirty miles south of here. I'll be mindful not to keep the connection open long enough for them to triangulate on our location. But they'll know everything they'll need to know; who they should expect will show up, where and when the meeting will take place, what they can expect to find in that yellow van, and they'll know that their people need to arrive in a white van with tinted windows. All the rest of it lies in their court. Oh, what I would give to watch it all go down this afternoon! If the feds weren't looking for me, too, I'd be tempted to go and ask them for a reward."

"And having the goods on El Tirano would be worth quite a nice monetary reward, that's for sure," Jessica remarked. "But I'll receive all the reward I will ever want anyway if our plan ultimately works. For me that's a lot more important than any amount of money."

She looked up the phone number for that FBI office in the City of Homestead on her phone and then handed the phone to Dugan to make the call. After he relayed the pertinent details to the federal agent who took the call and asked him to read the information back to him to ensure everything was copied accurately, he hung up before being pressed to answer any questions he knew would be asked of him.

A half hour later he and Jessica stood in the soft warm sand on one of the least populated and quietest sections of Miami Beach, and she pitched her phone out as far as she could into the surf to dispose of it. The ocean breeze swept over them and Dugan noticed Jessica's hair, even though it was shorter now since it had been cut to alter her appearance, fluttered like fluffy down feathers in the breeze. Her bright blue eyes shimmered in the sunlight, contrasted against the lightly suntanned skin of her forehead and cheeks. The scene etched its image into his brain that he was certain he would never be able to forget.

Then she and Dugan went to buy two new prepaid phones and also a portable radio with which they could monitor the news. The arrest of El Tirano along with several of his henchmen and the taking down of his huge crime organization would certainly be a major news story nationally. But the story wouldn't break until the next morning.

Suddenly they both faced the realization that they had fully accomplished what they had come to Florida to accomplish, and now they started feeling the itch to get out of town. They both had a growing sense that the whole area around Miami offered only danger for them now.

Jessica reassured Dugan that she still needed the services of a bodyguard, even though her main objective that she needed his help with seemed to have been concluded. The big question now was where to go and what to do. She hadn't really planned her future beyond the disruption of the international human trafficking ring.

Dugan didn't particularly want to go back to North Carolina right away. He knew there'd be federal agents all over around Fayetteville looking for him and for Jessica and they'd still be watching his uncle's farm.

Jessica finally suggested that they drive out to Texas and pay a brief visit to Dugan's parents.

"I'm dying to meet your mom and dad," she told him.

"I have no doubts that they'd find you perfectly charming, but I wonder if it's such a good idea. I mean, how long would it take for them to discover who you really are and about your abilities? As soon as they did there'd be little or no chance of talking Dad out of publishing a paranormal piece about it. His whole career has been wrapped around trying to find phenomena the likes of which you, um, well, all of those rare characteristics that you embody. If you knew my dad, he wouldn't be able to resist such a story. I'm not joking. I don't think you'd want that kind of publicity."

"Most of the people I meet and talk to never even have a clue about the things I'm able to do, or even suspect for a second that I'm reading their thoughts. I've got years of practice keeping my own secret, you know."

"Okay then. It's your call. Just don't say I didn't warn you if you dig yourself into a whole you can't climb out of."

CHAPTER 19

Again, as we reported in the previous hour the breaking news story this morning out of Southern Florida comes from WKMI News Matters' local affiliate in Miami. We'll bring you updates as new information becomes available, but what we know at this time is that what appears to be the largest rescue of kidnapping victims in North America in possibly decades happened late last night near Miami. At least thirty-three teenage girls and reportedly seven boys of ages ranging from nine to twelve who were being held captive in a warehouse by human traffickers were all safely rescued by law enforcement some time before midnight.

What has been confirmed by local authorities is that the rescue operation followed an exchange of gunfire earlier in the evening that killed three of the kidnappers and critically wounded two others, and apparently twelve other members of this international trafficking ring based in Miami – including the supposed ring leader - were arrested on multiple charges. It is being reported that the FBI acted on an anonymous tip that led to the dramatic arrests and rescue.

Please continue to stay tuned as we follow the latest developments on this gripping story throughout the day.

Dugan and Jessica were quiet - their attention was glued to the broadcast blaring from the car's radio as they traveled west on I-20. He had turned up the volume in the middle of the news update, and then after they had heard all of the details they had been waiting for, he turned the radio off.

Mission accomplishment had now finally been confirmed, and they shared a huge sense of relief. They had spent a couple hours tuned into a local news station on their new portable radio in the motel room last night, but the story broke this morning for the first time.

Jessica was driving. She still wanted to get in as much practice driving as she could, and Dugan didn't protest - it gave him another opportunity to relax a little and enjoy the ride and scan the scenery along the way. He still couldn't get over her demonstrated driving skill. She handled the lane changes, the merging with traffic and maintaining a safe interval between cars, and using turn signals as needed with total confidence. It was as if she'd been driving for years. She finally broke the silence.

"Shouldn't you call your dad and tell him we're coming to visit so your parents will be expecting us when we arrive?"

"Was kind of thinking about surprising them. They've always seemed to enjoy that kind of surprise whenever I've just showed up unannounced after they haven't seen me for a while."

"But this will be the first time I will be with you."

"That's true. And naturally they'll be curious about you. And they'll be curious about what our relationship is."

"What are you going to tell them?"

"I really don't know what to tell them. I mean, do I tell them the truth that I'm working for you as your bodyguard? That will definitely prompt further curiosity and then we'd have a bunch more explaining to do."

"Why not just tell them we're romantically involved?"

"You want me to lie to my parents?"

"Would it *really* be a lie? Don't forget I read your thoughts, Dugan, so I know all about your infatuation with me, which I know is actually a bit more than only that. You've tried to hide it but I know. Besides, we're great together. We make a perfect team and we'd make a great couple."

"I know you hate hearing this again and again but you're just too young for any guy my age. I was still in high school at seventeen, and my ten-year high school reunion was already a year ago! I was almost twelve years old when you were born!"

"You're worried about what other people will think, Dugan, like your parents. That's what you're really worried about."

"Maybe you're right, but we both know there's a lot more to it than that. Can people even really know what they want in life by age seventeen?"

"Sure, I think some can. And some people never figure out exactly what they really want in life, not ever. I at least know how you feel about me - that's one thing I do know. Another thing I know is how I feel about you. But if you're going to hold out for a more 'mature' woman you might be a long time looking."

"What if I'm just not ready for a relationship with anyone at this point in my life, no matter how perfectly suitable we might be for each other?"

"Well, it's not like I'm saying we should get married anytime soon or anything like that, although in reality we paid good money for papers that say we are husband and wife right now."

"Yeah, I guess we're kind of in that dimension right now more or less, aren't we? Where we should take everything from here is for me something of an open question. I can't go back to North Carolina anytime soon for obvious reasons. And I don't think we know of any other big crime organizations to dismantle and no more big challenges to keep us focused."

"Exactly. This just happens to be where we are with everything right now. And right now, I think you should call your dad and mom and let them know we're on our way. Whatever explanation you come up with about me I'll do my best to go along with it."

Dugan nodded and then retrieved his new phone from his pocket and proceeded to dial his parents' number.

"Hi Mom, how are you, and how's Dad?"

"Oh, we're both just fine, Dugan. This is such a coincidence. We were just talking about you."

"Well, I'm headed out to Texas right now for a short visit - planning to arrive sometime tomorrow evening. Did the truck and camper I told Dad about arrive yet?"

"Yes, it arrived day before yesterday. Hey, Dugan, are you in any kind of trouble right now?"

"No, not exactly. Why are you asking me that kind of question?"

"Yesterday two men stopped by the house asking lots of questions about you, like where they might find you and whether or not we knew anything about a certain teenage girl they're also looking for. They identified themselves as federal agents from Homeland Security. How would you be involved in whatever they were talking about? Who is this girl they mentioned?"

"It's kind of complicated, Mom. Those men may not even have been who they said they were, but it's impossible to know for sure. A lot of things aren't what they seem, though. What exactly did they say about why they're looking for me, or for that girl?"

"That's what's so strange. They wouldn't divulge hardly anything at all. Whatever the girl knows they're treating it as classified information."

"Dugan," his dad was now also on the line, "What exactly is going on, Son? I just now took the kitchen wastebasket outside and emptied it into the trash barrel along the side of the house, and I noticed the same gray van parked across the street that was parked in that same spot last night. The windows are darkly tinted so I couldn't see if anyone was in it. Vans like that with tinted windows never park on our quiet little cul-de-sac. I think they might be watching our house, whoever is looking for you.

"Whatever this is all about, Dugan, I don't think you should tell us about it over the phone, at least not right now. Never know who might be listening in. And this might be too risky of a time for you to visit us here, if we're being watched like it appears we are. Just watch your back, Son. Promise me you'll watch your step and lay low for a while, at least until whatever is going on now cools down. Check back in with us when you can. Your mother and I will naturally be worried sick until we hear from you and you know we will. But avoid the temptation to call us before you think it's safe."

"No matter whatever happens," his mother added, "just always remember that your dad and I love you very much, Dugan."

CHAPTER 20

"My team can eliminate Dugan Randall for you, Mr. Byrnell, but that isn't included with the price I quoted you just for delivering Jessica Knowles. This guy wasn't in the picture when we were negotiating the original deal, but we have to deal with him now. You'll definitely want for us to deal with him in this case, though, simply to avoid the potential headaches he could create for you. But making people disappear permanently costs more than a hundred K."

"How much more?"

The man paused before answering, "Half a million. Tack on an additional half million to the original price and Mr. Randall will never be an obstacle to you or to anyone else ever again."

Tony Byrnell shook his head, "This changes everything. We're working within a particular budget and that's a lot of money we haven't budgeted for. I don't have the authority to approve any changes that big, so I'll need to consult with the boss about it."

"That's perfectly understandable. Another possibility is to simply destroy her trust in him, which would effectively separate the two if it's done correctly, and then she'd be at least temporarily unguarded and easier pickings. My guys are very good at this sort of thing – at destroying someone's credibility in someone else's eyes."

"I don't believe that is at all possible in this situation given how she's a mind-reading psychic who would be able to see right through any plot like that. It would never work - you'll need a better plan."

The man appeared to be contemplating other possibilities. "We could very easily set him up to be arrested for something. He'd be out of the action if he were to be detained by authorities, at least for the amount of time we need."

"That idea sounds more workable for sure. So how much extra would that cost?"

"For a total of two hundred K we could create the scenario that would separate the two of them and we could grab Miss Knowles as soon as she's separated from her bodyguard and deliver her safely to you. Setting it all up could take a few more days than if we were to simply eliminate the guy, but it would be much more fun for us and less costly for you."

"You'll have to find them first. Do you even know where they are right now? You told me two days ago in our last meeting that your team lost them in Florida. Maybe I'm the one being conned – conned right out of two hundred thousand dollars!"

"It's true that they dropped off our radar for a short blip in Miami, but just yesterday afternoon they've turned up again, this time in Longview, Texas. We've got them in our sights for the moment, but it probably won't be too long before the feds catch up with them and that will definitely complicate the whole deal."

"How was your team able to find them again so quickly that far from Florida when even the whole Department of Homeland Security with all of its vast resources searching in earnest for over a week apparently still hasn't found them? How is that possible?"

"I'm sure you can appreciate that the details are a trade secret, but let's just say it involves access to the data base of the government's thousands of surveillance camera feeds from across the country and the image filtering and face recognition analysis in real time. NSA developed and manages the software that processes it all. For our business it helps to have one of our own people working in the program and having access to the data, since their system firewalls are so damned good that nobody ever hacks into it.

"But what matters most to our clients, Mr. Byrnell, is that we're in the people finding business, among other things. We've always been a forward-planning business that has literally spent years putting our own highly specialized people into certain strategic positions to help us achieve our goals. You might say we've learned how to apply the tools of the trade as we've managed to stay one step ahead of Homeland Security in this case."

A doubting grin flashed across Tony Byrnell's face, "Sounds like pure fantasy right out of a James Bond movie to me. I was hired for my present position at A.I. Technologies largely because I'm pretty good at spotting a con job and keeping the corporation out of these endless traps.

"And quite honestly this looks like a total con job to me, but I'll tell you what we're willing to do. You get Randall out of the picture and deliver Jessica Knowles to us in good health and we'll transfer the two hundred thousand to an account at a bank of your choice. But we're not paying one penny extra for anything else you might think up, not for babysitters, not for medical examinations, no storage fees, no handcuff surcharges or anything else! We don't care what you have to do to bring her to us. We'll pay only the two hundred thousand, and you'll receive the money only when we have received what we're paying for."

"We require half down upon the mutual agreement of any deal."

"Then we clearly don't have any deal. We'll have to find us another contractor."

The man sighed, "Okay, Mr. Byrnell, we'll make an exception and work under your terms this one time. Anyway, there is no other contractor that can do what we can do. You'll find that I have an extraordinary team that can make just about anything happen. We always deliver."

Tony Byrnell shook his head expressing his skepticism, "Well we'll find out if that's true, won't we? I just don't think you have the slightest concept of what Jessica Knowles is all about."

CHAPTER 21

Their heightened state of anxiety after Dugan's conversation with his parents kept Dugan and Jessica from being able to relax at the moment.

"They're watching my parents' house!" Dugan wailed. "My parents! Why does any of this have to involve *them*?"

"It doesn't involve them directly, not really. You and I both know that your parents are merely viewed as the bait that could lure you in. You and I are the prize fish they're fishing for and your parents are the only proverbial line in the water right now. They've got nothing else to go on at the moment."

"You think it's those Homeland Security guys doing the watching?"

"Yes, I do. And I wouldn't be surprised if your dad's suspicion about his landline being wiretapped ended up being accurate as well. I imagine government agencies tend to get the warrants they need."

"Something else is bothering you, too, I can tell. I guess this is what you get for teaching me how to read another's thoughts."

She gave him a surprised look. "I should have been prepared for that. So, how much of my thinking did you read?"

"Enough to know you're worried that someone we don't want knowing where we are knows where we are."

"You're a good reader. I haven't quite deciphered how they know where we are, but they do."

"Who are they this time?"

"Well, I don't believe it's anyone from the federal government. I'm pretty sure we're somehow being tracked by a private contractor. And I have a pretty strong sense they're working for that corporation I told you about that wants me for their secret science project. My sense is really strong at the moment and it's telling me we're being monitored."

The two of them were outside in a city park sitting at a picnic table, eating the lunch they'd brought with them and having a picnic. The weather had been sunny and hot, but the table was under a huge maple tree that provided excellent shade. It was early enough on a weekday that there weren't a lot of other people in the park yet. Dugan counted a total of seven other people scattered about the park.

He looked around them, "You mean they're watching us right now?"

Jessica nodded, "That's the feeling I'm getting, and like I said it's a strong feeling."

A subtle movement in a cluster of bushes between the trees across the park caught Jessica's attention. She watched the spot curiously for a moment, at first thinking it might be a dog or other animal. Right away the movement seemed to stop, but in another instant she caught a flash of sunlight being reflected off of a mirror-like object in that area. She realized it could be a dead giveaway of an optical lens like those of binoculars.

"How did they find us already?" Dugan wondered, trying to remember every step they had taken to throw all possible trackers off their trail. "What did we miss?"

"I believe we were picked up on surveillance cameras. I don't remember seeing any wherever we went, but I wasn't exactly looking too hard for them. It's the only possible explanation I can think of."

Dugan nodded, "I think you're right, and I didn't notice any cameras, either, but it makes sense. The only thing about it

I find odd is that someone other than the government could have access to the camera footage. How could a private contractor have access to that kind of data?"

"I don't know. But I think we're being spied on this very moment from those bushes to the right of that swing set and maybe a hundred or so yards behind it." She was careful not to nod or point in that direction. "They're just watching us and waiting for something they're planning to happen."

Dugan acknowledged discretely, resisting the temptation to look in the same direction.

Immediately they both noticed a man who was acting suspiciously slowly approach a couple of women sitting on a park bench probably no more than fifty yards away. While the two women seemed to be having a private conversation and basically ignoring the guy, he walked over to them and grabbed one of their purses. The woman with the purse turned around to face him and began to stand up when he shoved her over backwards and started running off with her purse.

Dugan instinctively sprang to his feet to chase the man down but Jessica managed to grab his arm and restrained him before he could free himself from the table. "It's a ruse, Dugan! You don't want to go anywhere near those women. The whole thing is a setup just to draw you into it."

"What are you talking about?" Dugan paused to think. "That guy is getting away with that lady's purse!"

"No, he's not. The whole thing was staged. They're betting you'll rush over to help and get yourself involved. Those women have been paid to ID you as the perpetrator when the police show up. You'll be arrested for robbery and assault. It's a total setup. Those are actors."

"You sure of that?"

"I am now," she looked over at the two women who seemed unusually calm following such an incident. "It's a ploy to get you out of the way. Their plan involves using the police to get you out of the way by arresting you for some fake crime. I should have read the signs before now. The clues were all there."

Dugan and Jessica wasted little time packing up their picnic supplies and leaving the park. They passed the arriving patrol car on their way out. This time Dugan was driving.

"How could they know we'd be at that park this morning?"

"I don't think they had any idea where we'd be before we ended up there, but they've been tracking us," she said. "They watched us enter the park, and they've had everything ready to go for wherever we might stop. I would bet money they even made a 9-1-1 call a few minutes before acting out their little caper to ensure the police would arrive in a timely manner."

"Are they tracking us right now?"

"I'm getting a strong feeling that they are."

Dugan was quiet for a few minutes while he drove. Overtly his mind appeared to be focused on his driving, but Jessica knew better. She didn't say anything. She was also rolling a myriad of conflicting thoughts through her head, struggling with something she knew she had to do but didn't want to do. He finally broke the silence.

"They'll be trying something like this again, won't they? I'm sure it'll be some totally different scenario since the first one failed, but…"

"Yes. They will. And they'll keep trying until they eventually succeed. Somebody is paying somebody else a lot of money to separate us. They believe they can deal with me more easily if I'm alone, and they have no qualms whatsoever about destroying a good guy like you if you're in their way. I know we've talked about it before, but it's only going to get worse."

"Yeah, well they would be right about having an easier time of it if they could get me out of the game, but I'm not going to let that happen. I'm staying in the game. I won't let them get their hands on you, Jessie. You know you can trust me about that."

"I know you won't, Dugan. I'm not worried about that at all - there was never any question in my mind about your ability to protect someone, and you've proved that more than once. That isn't the problem here.

"Hey, do you think we could we stop somewhere along here where it's kind of rural and quiet, and just talk? Maybe you could pull off the road right up ahead there under those huge trees where it's shady? I don't think quite as clearly when I'm moving."

"No problem," he said, slowing the car and pulling off the road where she requested before stopping and turning off the engine.

"I can't even imagine finding a better bodyguard than you, Dugan, and I know you realize that. But these people won't stop at one failed attempt, or even at two or three attempts. They will continue to stalk us. They will continue scheming and laying their traps. It would only be a matter of time until…"

"So what are you suggesting?"

She was suddenly quiet. She didn't know exactly how to answer the question. She hated the logical obvious answer to the question. Just the thought of her and Dugan going their separate ways was starting to make her feel sick inside.

"You know how I feel about you, Dugan, and you know I also know exactly how you feel about me. But what kind of life is this? I've been forced to survive this way for longer than I even want to remember, but it was very wrong for me to pull you into my treacherous world like I've done. And look at what is happening with your parents, Dugan - your involvement with me has people spying on your parents! Nobody would ever intentionally subject the people they care about to this kind of life."

"Are you trying to say you're firing me?"

"Not 'firing' – *saving*. Before it's completely too late - before your life is completely ruined beyond repair as you and I both know would eventually happen, I absolutely must cut you free from my hellish world, Dugan. Please know I'm very serious when I say there's nothing in this whole universe I could possibly ever hate worse than having to do this, but it's for the better. You know I'm right. There is no future for you with me – you even told me so yesterday – you said we're not right for each other because of our age difference, remember?

"So if we go our separate ways... if we go our separate ways *completely* so that you don't have any idea about where to find me or how to contact me, that is the only way we can do this. Oh, they'll continue to watch you for a while no doubt, and you might expect some interrogation but I don't believe they'll harm you, or at least I pray that they won't. But these people will eventually leave you alone when they figure out you can't lead them to me. It's that simple. And then you can have your life back."

"No, it's not 'that simple'. What life did I have before I met you? Sure, I've understood from the beginning that this was only a temporary job. I'm okay with the *job* coming to an end. I can find another job. But you've become a lot more to me than just an employer, Jessie. You know what I mean. I won't leave you to face your burden all by yourself. I won't do that. I *can't* do that. We'll survive or we'll fall together. We're the perfect team you and I – you even said so yourself! We can continue with what we've been doing, working together to make the world a better place. What could be better than that?"

"We've had this conversation too many times already, Dugan, and I've had plenty of time to consider everything.

Now I've made up my mind and you're not going to change it. Goodbye, Dugan," she said in a quivering voice as she opened the passenger door and stepped out of the vehicle with her gym bag slung over her shoulder. She wouldn't make direct eye contact with him but he nevertheless noticed her watery eyes. He couldn't remember ever seeing tears in her eyes before. "Please don't try to follow me," she added. "I pray you'll stay safe and keep yourself out of trouble and live the life I want you to live, the life you deserve. But please let me just go my own way."

Dugan noticed she'd left her phone on the passenger's seat. He almost yelled to let her know about it, but he quickly understood that her leaving her phone behind was intentional. She didn't want him trying to call her. He helplessly watched her as she walked away from the car until she vanished into the shadows of the tree line.

CHAPTER 22

Dugan sat in the driver's seat of the Equinox for more than a moment just trying to decide exactly what he should do. His senses were numb. He wanted to go run after her and plead with her, but something made him hesitate. Maybe it was the knowledge that doing so would be against her wishes. Maybe it was that he knew down deep he wouldn't change her mind with all of the pleading he could muster.

He opened the driver's side door and stepped out onto the gravel and weeds. This was a quiet country road. He gazed into the trees where Jessica had disappeared. He could see nothing other than trees and leafy branches and the darkness of the shade and shadows among the eastern Texas trees.

"Jessica!!!" he yelled her name as loud as he could and then listened, but heard no response. "Can't we just talk about this? I really have no life without you now and you know it's true. Let's just talk okay, Jessie?"

He waited. He listened. The trees were quiet. He wondered how far she could have gone in the minute or so that had transpired since she'd left. She couldn't have gone far. She would still be within range of his shouting. But he knew deep down that it was all in vain. She wasn't going to answer him. She wasn't coming back. She was gone.

He got back into the car and just sat in the driver's seat. A thousand different thoughts seemed to be racing through his head all at the same time. He wasn't eager to start the car and drive off right away. To just leave right now seemed like the wrong thing to do. But how long should he stay here? It was still possible that she could change her mind and return to the car, though he knew the chance of that happening was extremely small. Nevertheless, an extremely small chance *was still a chance.*

He couldn't stop reflecting back over all of their conversations earlier in the day and trying to remember whatever she'd said that might've been a hint about all of this that he had missed. And he couldn't stop wondering how he might have possibly talked her out of leaving had he only had any inkling that this was what she was going to do.

But no answers came to him. He didn't even have Jessica's sometimes inconsistent ability to read the future so he couldn't have predicted any of this. He hadn't read any such message in her thoughts at all. And Jessica leaving him like this was the last thing in the world he would ever have expected.

He hadn't yet started the ignition when he noticed the approaching black vehicle in his side mirror. It pulled off the road onto the shoulder right behind the Equinox.

Dugan decided against driving away immediately. Doing so might have been the wisest thing to do under the circumstances, but his curiosity got the better of him.

Two men exited the car and approached the Equinox. Dugan looked at his watch. Barely ten minutes had passed since Jessica had walked off into the trees. If these guys were after her he would need to do everything he could to delay or distract them to buy her as much time as possible.

He slowly stepped out of the Equinox and his right hand instinctively reached discretely behind him until his fingers found the grip of the HK P30 that he had appropriated from one of the men he'd killed.

"No reason for that, Mr. Randall. We're not looking for a gunfight. People get hurt in gunfights. We just want to have a friendly chat with you, that's all."

"Who are you guys?"

"Who we are isn't quite as important as what we want," one of them said.

"Or," the other said, "what we're willing to pay you for helping us get what we want."

Dugan's trained mind began assessing the details of the situation. He made quick mental estimates of the distance between the two men, their distance from him, where their concealed weapons were most likely positioned under their jackets, their expressed level of confidence and body language, what kinds of strategies for action might seem logical from their perspective... He noticed the front license plate on their car looked (from where he stood, anyway) like an Illinois plate. This and the fact that they had implied a willingness to pay cash for what they wanted were strong clues that these men weren't federal agents.

"You guys want Jessica Knowles."

The closest one nodded, "It's just business."

"And I suppose you wouldn't believe me if I told you I don't happen to know where she is at the moment."

"You're right, we wouldn't believe you. We know the two of you have been traveling together for more than a week. She's probably just sitting there in your car right now."

"Feel free to have a look inside for yourself – the doors aren't locked. As you guys probably already know I've been working for her as her bodyguard, until this morning anyway. But she's informed me that she no longer needs a bodyguard, and so I am once again unemployed."

While he was explaining all of this, one of the men inspected the inside of his car. Then he looked under the car and scanned the surroundings.

"Okay, so she's not here. So where *is* she?"

"Earlier she mentioned a cousin who lives in Huntsville. I offered to drive her down there but she didn't want to pay me anything for my gas. She'd rather spend more taking a taxi I guess. Female logic, right? Anyway, I left her alone back at the park we visited a little earlier since she no longer needs a bodyguard. It was her choice, not mine."

"Why is your car stopped way out here on this lonely road?"

"I needed a quiet place to just sit and think about things. I have a few things to sort out before I go anywhere, like where will I go from here, you know?"

The men looked understandably skeptical but they knew they presently had no other leads to follow.

"We'll look into it, Randall, but if your story doesn't wash, we'll come see you again. We know how to find you, and it'll be a very different conversation we'll be having the next time if we do."

Dugan gave a sigh of relief right after the two men drove away. Jessica wasn't going to be tracked from this point, at least not right now, and not by these two men. Dugan had had to get creative on the spot with his improvisation for a diversion, but it seemed to have worked for the time being.

He still didn't want to drive away yet. Rational thinking told him Jessica was long gone by now, and she wasn't coming back. Nevertheless, it seemed so wrong to leave this place – to just drive off and leave the place where he and Jessica conversed for their last time. He still considered following her trail in hopes of catching up with her and at least try to talk some sense into her, but again rational thinking told him it was hopeless. Jessica was possibly the strongest-willed individual he had ever known. Besides, if she had any intentions of returning to the car she would have returned already.

He thought about the long and lonely drive he would have back to North Carolina. It would give him a lot of time to think and contemplate his own future from this point forward.

There would be plenty to deal with once he was back in North Carolina. There would be government people and others hounding him as soon as he returned no doubt, and he still had to move all of his worldly possessions out of his uncle's barn and into a storage facility in Fayetteville. He knew some old friends he could call to help him move everything. After all of that it would be back to job hunting again.

CHAPTER 23

Jessica emerged from the thicket roughly half a mile from where she said goodbye to Dugan. By this time her eyes were so filled with tears she could barely see some of the leafy tree branches she had to push her way through, and she tripped a few times, almost twisting her ankle once.

    The weather was hot and muggy. She could feel her shirt clinging to her sweaty skin and her throat was dry and burning, but she wasn't focused on these physical annoyances. She was almost oblivious to most of them in her state of grief. At this point she was experiencing such emotional misery that she almost wished she were dead.

    As she wandered out into the clearing, she suddenly realized she was likely on private property. Some distance away, possibly a couple hundred feet from her across the open field was a woman wearing a straw hat working in her garden. The woman had looked up, apparently to see who or what was stumbling out of the tree line.

    Jessica suddenly felt a dizziness sweep over her like a wave and the last thing she remembered was a brief sense of falling.

    She came to consciousness maybe just a few minutes later as the woman wearing the hat was placing a folded wet hand towel over her forehead to cool her down. Without turning her head, Jessica's eyes received enough scenery that she knew this was the same spot where she had collapsed. The gym bag strap was still draped over her shoulder and the bag was at her side undisturbed.

The woman with the hat had darker skin and appeared to Jessica to be either Native-American or of Latin-American heritage, and maybe about fifty to sixty years old. She retrieved a bottle of water from her small ice cooler she had with her when she noticed that Jessica was awake, and she unscrewed the cap before handing it to her.
    "How are you feeling?" the woman asked her.
    "Okay I guess," Jessica sat upright, holding the damp cloth to her head with one hand and receiving the bottle of water with the other, and then took a long sip of water. "Thank you! Where am I?"
    "Harrison County, Texas. This little field of tall grass is just part of our forty-acre timber ranch that my husband and I own. People around here call it the Fuentes Ranch, because our last name is Fuentes. I have my little hobby garden over there, and our home is on the other side of that stand of trees near the garden. It's kind of hard to see from here. When I noticed you coming out of the timber line I thought you were a deer at first," the woman didn't speak with any sort of Mexican or Latino accent at all, but instead with a vaguely distinguishable Texas drawl.
    "I apologize for trespassing. I honestly didn't even know I was on private property, really."
    "No worries, Hun. It's nice to have a new visitor once in a while, anyhow. Hey, are you lost, or maybe running away from someone who's trying to harm you?"
    "I think I'm trying to run away from myself, actually. It's all very complicated."
    "Well, let's get you over to the house where you can relax a spell and cool off in the air-conditioned atmosphere - maybe drink some iced tea, how about that? The thought of a cold glass of iced tea sure appeals to me, anyway. I've been out here in the sun for close to half an hour already and it's making me hotter than a two-dollar pistol. Of course, the hat's

shade helps a lot, but I'm still spittin' cotton already and I imagine you must be, too. Do you think you're okay to walk?"

"Yes, ma'am, I believe so," Jessica rose to her feet.

"Okay, we'll just mosey on over to the house slowly in case another dizzy spell grabs hold of ya. My name is Isabella, by the way."

"I'm Jessica. Thanks for helping me, Isabella."

The Fuentes' home was a majestic Spanish-style rancher with wide archways, beige-white stucco siding, and an orange-brown tiled roof. They obviously had no close neighbors - no other homes were visible from here. By Jessica's best visual estimate just from looking at the entryway and front living room plus the outside from the front, this house must've had easily over four thousand square feet of living space. Isabella's husband, Carlos, owned a construction company she explained. He had run his business for twenty-five years but was planning to retire within the next two years.

Jessica liked this woman right away. Her friendly personality wasn't so much a conscious disposition, but rather it was simply the natural expression of who she really was. She was easy for Jessica to read – easy for Jessica to recognize that her generosity was genuine and that her concern for others was powerful.

"We never had any children," Isabella said, handing Jessica a tall glass of ice-cold tea and then gesturing for her to take a seat at a small breakfast table in the spacious kitchen, "because we were both so doggone busy all the time when we were younger. We've become financially very 'comfortable' over the years with his construction business and my sales commissions from selling real estate from which I finally retired last year, but sometimes I sure do wish we had children, and it's kind of too late for that now.

"Carlos and I still have some great friends who mostly live in Marshall with whom we get together with from time to time and he has two brothers who still live over in El Paso where we're both from – where we both grew up and went to school together, but not a lot of other family to speak of.

"What about you, Jessica? You don't sound like you're from Texas. Do you have any family around here?"

Jessica instinctively hesitated and then immediately realized she could safely confide in this woman about anything and everything, if specific questions were asked of her.

"No. You're right I'm not from Texas. I was actually born in Nevada but I've lived in a lot of different places. I was raised by my dad since my mom didn't survive my birth, and I didn't have any siblings. My dad passed away almost a year ago, so I've been on my own for a while."

Isabella took a sip of tea and didn't immediately respond, having no words in her mind in the moment she considered worth uttering besides finally, "I am so sorry."

Jessica could read her sympathetic thoughts as well as her awkward feeling about having brought up the topic of family in that instance. Scanning her surroundings for something to prompt a change in conversation, Jessica noticed a small table in the adjoining parlor with two chairs and a chess board on it.

"Do you play chess very often?"

Isabella nodded, "Carlos loves the game and he's very good at it. He finally taught me how to play about.., maybe four years ago - something like that. We'll usually play two or three games a week these days. It's kind of a stress reliever for him, I think. It's an effective way to get the mind off of other things. What about you, Jessica? Do you play?"

"I've never actually tried it."

"Oh, I could teach you the basics of the game in about fifteen minutes I think if you'd like to learn."

"You mean right now?"

"Sure, why not? I don't have anything more important to do at the moment, do you?"

"No, I guess I don't. Okay then, yes I would love to learn how to play chess."

Jessica followed Isabella to the table upon which the chess board rested with all of the pieces of the set, and they took their seats at the opposite ends of the table.

"To start with," Isabella said, "the board should be positioned just like it is here, with a light square in the lower right corner on both playing ends of the board. We each start with sixteen pieces; one player has all black pieces and the other has all white. For this game I'll be white and you'll be black. So, we each have eight pawns, two rooks (they're the ones that look like little castle towers), two bishops, one king and one queen, and two knights (the horses)."

"Is this anything at all like checkers? I used to play checkers with my dad almost daily most of the time I was growing up. It was always frustrating for him because he could never beat me at it!"

"Well, that means you're a strategic thinker and that's exactly what you need to be when you play chess. It's all about strategy – about always looking ahead to how a possible scenario might play out. But chess and checkers are two different buckets of possums, as you'll soon find out. In chess, the different pieces have completely different kinds of moves that they can make. So, the rules are definitely more complicated for chess than they are for checkers.

"For example, in this game a pawn moves forward one space at a time (except on its first move it can move two spaces) but it can capture another piece diagonally, whereas a queen can move as far as she can go in any direction, but she may not skip over or past any of her own pieces. A knight, on the other hand, moves in the shape of an L - two spaces in one direction and then one space at a ninety-degree angle – and it can also jump over other pieces. Bishops move diagonally as far as they can go. Rooks move forward, backward, or sideways as far as they can go, but never diagonally. Your king is the piece you want to protect. He can never actually be captured, but a situation that *threatens* the king with capture is called 'check', and when there's no way to remove the threat, it's called 'checkmate'. That's when the game is over."

Most of the first game was played with a lot of questions from Jessica as might be expected. But Isabella discovered almost immediately that Jessica learned the rules and strategies remarkably fast, and as the game progressed it also became apparent that the girl remembered all of the details she had been taught as well as coming up with some of her own surprising strategies. Jessica won the first game handily and she was already well in the lead in the second game, having captured five pieces while sacrificing only one pawn, plus reaching the other side with her first pawn and having it promoted to a second queen.

"You weren't just pulling my leg about having never played chess before, were you?"

"No ma'am. I've played checkers more times than I can count, but never chess before today. That's the honest-to-God truth."

"Well, I wish I could just say that you're having beginner's luck, Jessica, but I suspect there's a bit more going on here than just luck. Am I right?"

"Yes, you're right in the sense that luck doesn't have much to do with it. I'm just a really fast learner, that's really all there is to it. I've always been a very fast learner."

Jessica surveyed the room looking for a Bible or a phone book or any other book or magazine with pages of printed words, but she didn't happen to see any in this room.

"You could show me a page or two from any book or encyclopedia and allow me no more than one minute to read it, and then quiz me on what I've read. I think you'd be surprised. And I know that it's bad manners to boast about these things, but I *am* able to speak four languages (including Spanish and English) with almost an equal degree of fluency."

"¿Puedes tener una conversación conmigo en Español completamente?"

"¡Claro que si! ¿De que le gustaría hablar?"

Isabella raised her eyebrows, "Well I'm impressed! My own heritage is presumably Mexican but I was adopted by Gringo Texican parents before the age of three (they were the two angels in my life) and I grew up speaking English at home. Carlos's parents on the other hand (and his grandparents) were from Mexico and they spoke only Spanish in their home. I took Spanish in high school and in college, but most of what I've learned about the language I learned over the last two decades from my husband.

Isabella then looked at Jessica curiously, "You were born with this ability to learn and remember things like this?"

"I believe so. You could test me on something, anything you can think of."

"Girl, you just learned how to play chess and this is only your second game in your whole life and already you're capturing all my pieces without even half trying! And I'm not exactly a terrible player. I think you've already aced your first test as far as I'm concerned. Carlos doesn't usually get home before six most evenings but I can't wait to see the look on his face when he loses his first game to you!"

"Does this mean I'm invited to stay for dinner? Maybe I could help you with the cooking?"

"Yes! Please stay and have dinner with us (we tend to call it supper). And you're also welcome to spend the night here, too, if you don't have somewhere else you need to be. We have a comfortable guest bedroom. I am enjoying your company very much, Jessica, and I'd sure love to hear all about your life, or at least as much as you feel comfortable sharing."

"What shall we fix for supper then?"

"Do you like chili? Carlos loves my recipe for Texas-style chili and I haven't made any for weeks. Thinking about making a huge pot of it because you can't eat just one bowl - once you start eating it's really hard to stop. Pretty sure I have everything we'll need to make it; tomatoes, onions, ground beef, chili beans, all the spices... The onions and tomatoes are fresh from my garden."

"Chili sounds pretty good to me right now. Just the thought of it is making me really hungry," Jessica admitted.

"Well how about we get started on it right now then?"

Later after dinner (and after beating Carlos in two games of chess to the satisfaction of Isabella) Jessica shared a summary of her life's story with her new friend. And Isabella was the only person she had ever met - besides her late father and Dugan Randall - she felt comfortable trusting with her secrets.

Even then, she decided not to reveal totally *everything*. She couldn't see any benefit in trying to explain her psychic abilities to Isabella, at least not at this point anyway.

The recounting of recent events in her life refreshed her thoughts of Dugan. That was where the telling of her story became especially difficult for her, and she knew that Isabella detected as much.

"You describe this young man, Dugan, the way a woman describes a man she loves more than her own life."

"I would be lying if I tried to claim that I didn't," Jessica mumbled with suddenly wet eyes.

"And you did say you believe he's in love with you, too."

"That's what makes this so incredibly painful."

"What if you're wrong in your belief that his life would be in more danger with you than it will otherwise be without you? Wouldn't it be a tragedy if two people who shared the same feelings for each other – two people possibly *meant* to be together ended up going their separate ways all because of a potentially false assumption?"

"But what if it isn't a false assumption? What if I actually *do* bring danger to his life? How could I justify my selfishness if something bad ever happened to him because of me?"

"I understand your concern for the safety of someone you care deeply about, Jessica, and I believe it *is* definitely a valid concern. But you have a lot of other things to also consider here. I mean, can you guarantee yourself that Dugan's whole world won't be plagued with emptiness now without you? And likewise can you guarantee that your own world won't be empty without him? For all we know his life could be in just as much (or more) peril without you as it might be with you."

Jessica had asked herself all of these same basic questions and she had been torn by her inability to clearly answer them. Now hearing the questions coming from another person – from an adult she recognized as having possessed considerable wisdom, was moving her to second guess her decision to leave Dugan.

She spent the night at the Fuentes' and then the next morning after a warm shower and a hearty breakfast consisting of toast, bacon, and fried eggs, Isabella drove her to town just like she had offered to do the day before.

"I sure wish you weren't set on leaving so soon, but I understand you have to follow your own way. I do hope you'll give some serious thought to what we talked about last night, Jessica."

"I have, Isabella, believe me I have. And I can say with conviction that you've opened my eyes up a lot. I don't know how to express my gratitude for everything."

"Oh, the pleasure was mine, Dear. Wherever your road takes you and whatever you do, I pray it will be the right path for you and that the good Lord watches over you the whole way."

"I believe the good Lord guides me. He's been guiding me every step of the way all along."

"Please promise me you'll come back and see us again very soon (and often), won't you?"

"I promise."

Where Jessica was headed from Longview was anybody's guess. It was clear that she would be riding on a Greyhound bus, but she wasn't saying where she was ultimately headed because, in reality, she wasn't even sure herself at this point where her journey would take her. She only knew that she had to be getting on her way to wherever it was she was going, and the sooner the better.

CHAPTER 24

Dugan drove non-stop from East Texas to North Carolina, only pulling his car off the road once for about an hour's nap in his car roughly fifty miles west of Atlanta between one o'clock and two in the morning, when his eyes had become simply too tired to stay open any longer. He might have slept longer but something – he never figured out exactly what - woke him up. Once awake he felt the urge to continue on, as if he were in a race to his destination.

For the first time in a very long time he was overcome with a kind of irrational feeling he was not accustomed to, like a sense of desperation – desperation to return quickly to familiar surroundings. He'd been rolling recent events in his mind over again and again as he drove the first hundred miles, then another hundred miles, then three hundred and four hundred miles, and this was starting to get mentally exhausting.

He needed some kind of diversion. His thought was that familiar places and old friends might help him get his mind off of his experiences over the last couple of weeks, and he was suddenly anxious to return home.

He realized that he should expect the government surveillance to still be monitoring his old residence at the barn. They would surely be watching him from the moment he got back. Nevertheless, he still had some things to do there. He still had to move his personal belongings to a storage facility and clean out the barn by the deadline Sarah had given him.

Somewhere just beyond Greenville, South Carolina on I-85 he got the feeling the Equinox was being tailed. This time it didn't appear that just one vehicle was following him but at least two different vehicles seemed to be traveling continuously within view of the Equinox, suspiciously appearing to adjust their speed to his frequent changes in his cruising speed. Both of the vehicles were white in color; one looked like a Buick Enclave and the other probably a Chevy Traverse. He considered that either or both of them could easily be government vehicles. He couldn't be a hundred percent sure about it, but it seemed like a very unlikely coincidence if he were wrong.

Presently there didn't seem to be much he could do to lose them. It probably wouldn't have mattered anyway even if he could since anyone able to track his movements from one state to another at this point would no doubt also know the location of the barn, and he was headed there to take care of what he needed to take care of regardless.

Before returning to the barn, however, it seemed like a good idea to transfer the vehicle title and re-register the Equinox from Felix McAllister's name to Dugan Randall's. Unlike in Florida, in North Carolina this process was handled at the DMV, and Dugan had visited that office a number of times in the past so this time around he wouldn't have to bother looking anything up on his phone. He expected the waiting in line and the paperwork and all of it would be time-consuming but he didn't even care. It was just another errand on his long list of errands to eliminate - just another hoop to jump through in the course of slowly putting his life back on track.

He was running all of these things through his mind that would need to get done; renting a storage unit, renting a moving van, recruiting some friends to help him move some of his heaviest personal property like his gun safe and exercise machines. And he would need to get an apartment and find a new job.

It was decidedly too late in the day by the time he reached Fayetteville to tackle a bunch of errands. The DMV was already closed, but Dugan didn't want to show up at the barn in a vehicle with plates registered to a fictitious person named Felix McAllister. That would just open up a can of worms he didn't need to open up right now. He decided to get a room for the night at a motel where he would try to catch up on some of the sleep he'd lost.

But it was a restless night. He tossed and turned in the bed, woke up periodically in sweaty fits between unpleasant dreams and was never really able to completely get thoughts of Jessica out of his head. He couldn't shake the realization that he most likely would never see her again, and that was a much more difficult thing to think about than he ever would have imagined.

He had brought the guitar case into the motel room with him where he could keep an eye on it and have quick access to everything in it. He couldn't stop wondering about those two vehicles that had followed him. It was impossible to know who they were. He hadn't been able to see them anymore once he'd gotten within about ten miles of Fayetteville, but that didn't mean they weren't still tracking him. And just because he'd noticed two vehicles was no guarantee there weren't others he'd failed to notice.

The nagging bigger question Dugan couldn't answer was whether they knew where he was right now. Had he successfully evaded them up on the highway so that now they were scrambling to pick up his trail? That didn't seem likely, given how they had picked up his trail on the road in the first place. Besides, if they'd done their homework, they would surely know where the barn was outside of Fayetteville that he was residing in before this whole nightmare had begun for him.

    He couldn't help wondering if this kind of paranoia, either with merit or without, would be a permanent part of life for him from now on – just as it had been for Jessica for a number of years, or if there was any reasonable way to just ignore all of these unknown, unnerving possibilities and actually attempt living some kind of normal life.

    Another thing that had been bothering him since he'd encountered the two men in Texas was how anyone was ever able to track the Equinox in the first place. He couldn't think of any time when anyone would have had an opportunity to place a tracking chip somewhere in or on the vehicle. Nevertheless, he decided he would make a diligent search for that before heading over to the Department of Motor Vehicles in the morning. A good detective doesn't leave any stone unturned.

    The first rays of the morning sun were piercing the sky over the city's horizon when Dugan discretely peeked through the curtains of the motel room looking for those two white vehicles that he'd noticed tailing him the day before. There was no car resembling either one in the motel's parking lot or across the street where it would be visible from his room.

    He decided to go for a morning run. His exercise routine had become a kind of hit-and-miss activity over the last two weeks but he didn't want to let himself get completely out of shape. He also knew that a good run that got his blood flowing would help him clear his mind.

    Before he left, he wedged a tiny piece of folded paper inconspicuously between the door and the door frame six inches down from the top of the door such that it would fall free when the door was opened. When he returned from jogging this was the first thing he checked, to see if anyone had entered the room while he was out. To his relief the folded paper was still in the position where he had placed it. Out of habit he made sure the door was securely locked. He realized that the lock wouldn't be difficult for a professional to pick open, so he grabbed the room's one small desk chair and wedged its back firmly against the door. Looking around the room he found an empty metal wastebasket and he set it up on the chair. This makeshift obstacle he knew wouldn't actually block the door from a determined intruder, but it would most likely cause a noisy entry if anyone came in while Dugan was taking his morning shower.

From the guitar case Dugan removed his Glock 17 pistol with its full 17-round magazine, worked the slide to chamber a round and then removed the magazine to add one more live round before re-inserting it into the grip of the pistol. Eighteen rounds just seemed better than seventeen right now. He still had the HK P30 and it was also loaded with a full magazine, though with not quite as many rounds as were in the Glock. Both pistols would be in the bathroom with him while he showered, lying on the toilet tank lid within arm's reach from behind the shower curtain, just in case he heard any strange noises while he was in the bathroom.

He felt refreshed under the lukewarm stream of water rinsing away his sweat. For the first time in many hours, he was able to more or less mentally concentrate on his future without the pressing temptation to dwell on his recent past. It seemed he'd finally exhausted that temptation, and the water splashing onto his head in the moment seemed to symbolically wash away the recent past as well as wake his senses to his new direction. Wherever Jessie was now he believed she would most likely be looking to the future rather than continuously at the past. He imagined how she might be urging him to start a new private investigator business if she were here with him now. That had worked pretty well for him in the past.

But first things first. After checking out from the motel and eating breakfast at a fast-food place, he would visit the DMV as soon as they opened and take care of the vehicle registration. Once that was out of the way he would return to the barn and start packing up all of his belongings.

It was just before Noon when he returned to the barn. His eyes surveilled the trees along the driveway and across the property as he drove in, but he didn't see anyone and the area was quiet. Sarah's car was gone, but he knew she would be at work this time of day.

At first, he didn't spot anything out of the ordinary. Things appeared to be the way he'd left them the week before, at least on the outside. The many tire grooves in the gravel were probably made by the Jeep that he no longer owned. He'd never paid that much attention to those before. And he didn't see any obvious signs of forced entry.

When he checked the door knob, however, he found that the door was unlocked. That was an indication that someone had entered the building while he was gone, because he was always very careful to lock the door behind him whenever leaving his premises.

This suddenly begged a string of new questions. Who had gone inside his residence while he was out, and why? When were they here? Could someone still be inside right now waiting for him? The fact that he didn't see any vehicles on the property made him think it was unlikely there would still be anyone inside there.

Dugan came prepared for the worst. His Glock 17 quickly filled his right hand, and it still had a live round in the chamber. He crouched low to the ground and gently pushed the door open and counted silently to ten while straining his ears to listen for any sounds before cautiously going inside.

CHAPTER 25

Dugan found the barn unoccupied. And he found all of his personal belongings, including his exercise machines, gun safe containing the balance of his guns and ammo, his computer, television, refrigerator, furniture, clothing and everything else inside the barn undisturbed, just like he'd left it. The only logical explanation he could think of for the barn being entered while he was gone was that maybe Sarah started worrying about him after those Homeland Security guys had paid a visit and then he had disappeared shortly thereafter for nearly a week. She was the only other person who had a key to the door - that had been his own idea, making sure she had an extra key to his apartment in the barn just for emergencies. Perhaps she had let the authorities in if they'd been searching for him.

He conducted an exhaustive search of the whole premises for any possible hidden listening devices but didn't find any. He was also finally satisfied that the Equinox was free of any tracking devices after having first searched it briefly before leaving the motel parking lot, and then again more thoroughly after he had returned to the barn.

These efforts did little to reduce his own paranoia, however, and he wondered if his level of wariness might have been just a little excessive and perhaps not entirely necessary at this point.

Pondering all of these things made him remember how things used to be before Jessica had entered his world. Over the years he had grown accustomed to his privacy and the solitude this place had to offer. But now he felt there was something suddenly lonely about it. The surrounding trees were maybe a little too quiet now, *maybe*, although he hated to admit that to himself.

It was a challenge for him to get his mind off of Jessica at the moment and to focus his attention on all of the things he needed to do now. He had friends to call to ask for their help in moving his heavy things. At least that would be interacting with people, which was probably what he needed the most right now. He was well aware that it was going to take a conscious effort to move his life beyond his recent past.

By the third night after leaving Texas, he felt that he had finally put Jessica out of his mind, at least as much as he believed possible at this stage under the circumstances. Now he would be able to better concentrate on his future.

By this time, he had found a modest apartment available in Fayetteville and had already moved the bulk of his possessions with the help of two of his buddies he'd known since high school. It would be his first night spent in the new apartment and before sundown he had it furnished to his satisfaction, at least for the time being.

But what might otherwise have been a long and restful night of quality sleep - a much-needed full night of sleep - was interrupted just before three o'clock in the morning when he suddenly awoke from a bizarre dream in which Jessica appeared. After he woke up from that dream, he was never able to get back to sleep for the rest of the morning until daylight when he finally decided to force himself up out of bed.

In the dream Jessica had appeared as a larger-than-life angelic entity emerging from the clouds in the sky. She seemed to fly down from the clouds just to deliver her brief message to Dugan before quickly disappearing. Her lips didn't appear to move, but he clearly heard her words. She said to him, "Have patience, Dugan. Believe and be strong."

The image in the dream had seemed so incredibly vivid that it caused Dugan to wonder at first if he had actually been visited by Jessica's presence somehow. Then after lying awake for fifteen minutes pondering the dream that idea seemed utterly ridiculous. What actually *did* make sense, he realized, was that his thoughts of her were etched deeply into his sub-consciousness and it would be perfectly normal for them to manifest themselves in his dreams.

The words she'd spoken without moving her lips in the dream seemed rather odd to him. It felt as if someone was sending him a message, but if that were really the case then what were those words supposed to mean? *Have patience. Believe. Be strong.* Have patience for *what* exactly? Believe in *what*? The "message" didn't seem to make much sense even with the more plausible explanation of it merely originating from his own sub-consciousness. Where did those particular words come from?

A sense of guilt started nagging at him hard all of a sudden – guilt for having left Jessica alone in the woods without even attempting to go after her. He could have no assurances now of her well-being. For all he knew she could have stumbled across an aggressive black bear in the woods, or tripped on a log and maybe broken a leg or even her neck, or been bitten by a venomous snake, or God only knew what all could have happened to her while she was trekking through the woods all alone.

This was an ugly feeling that he couldn't shake and there wasn't anything he could realistically do about it now. In hindsight he didn't believe he would be deterred by her stubbornness were he given the chance for a do-over, knowing all the things that he had considered since. Had he gone into the woods after her like he now wished he had, at least he would've now had solace in the fact that he had done everything in his power to protect her, whether it had been against her wishes or not. He reminded himself once again that it was too late to do anything about it now.

He didn't want to take the time to go jogging this morning. He had too many other things - more pressing things to concern himself with he decided.

The barn had been basically cleaned out over the last couple days but Dugan still wanted to give it a final sweeping and last-minute inspection before handing the door key over to Sarah. He drove onto the graveled driveway just after 8:00 a.m. and parked close to the barn. As he stepped outside the Equinox, he immediately got the feeling he was being watched. Sarah had already gone to work so he knew they weren't her eyes studying his every move. It was a strong sense he had and, with or without merit it was definitely unnerving.

While still standing close to the Equinox his eyes briefly scanned the surrounding trees on the property, but nothing seemed out of place. The property was stone quiet without even the slightest breeze stirring any of the tree branches. Since his encounter with the two men outside of Longview he had made a habit of keeping his pair of binoculars on the passenger's seat for quick access instead of packed away in the guitar case where he'd stored them before.

In this moment he reached inside his car and grabbed the strap of the optic to have a better look at things. When he turned around with his binoculars in his hands, he saw two heavily armed men wearing camouflage and ski masks emerge from the woods, and in another instant two more appeared, also wearing masks so as to conceal their identities.

Dugan instinctively reached for his own concealed pistol but was swiftly warned against drawing it with stern words and the muzzle end of what appeared to be a suppressed

HK MP5. He decided to raise his arms with open hands to calm any possible itchy trigger fingers. His binoculars fell to the gravel.

"What do you guys want? I've moved everything I own with any real value to my new apartment sixteen miles away. You'll see when you look inside – not much left here for you."

"Don't be an idiot, Dugan Oliver Randall. You know we're not interested in your worthless crap."

One of them walked up behind him and disarmed him before he had time to thoroughly contemplate his predicament. Then that same guy punched him in the stomach hard enough to knock the wind out of him. It folded him over slightly, but he managed to stay on his feet. His eyes swept across the figures standing around him. His brain made split-second estimations of distances and calculations of potential moves plus their possible counter moves.

But it was no good. These men were spaced too far apart and they all had guns pointed at him, and there didn't happen to be only one or two men to deal with here, but *four* of them! Plus, they were most likely well aware of his own background – they knew who he was so they'd likely be prepared for whatever he might try to do. Obviously, these were professional thugs, probably just as well trained in martial arts as he was. An opportunity for a surprise move might eventually present itself at some point, but this clearly wasn't the right moment for that.

Before he could even second guess his assessment of the situation his hands were bound behind his back with multiple wrappings of duct tape while a pillow case was pulled over his head to blind him, and then a rope noose was drawn around his neck like a dog leash. He felt the barrel of a carbine jabbed into his rib cage and he was towed by the neck rope through the woods to some unknown destination.

As he stumbled and staggered through the woods being led with the rope, he tried his best to determine the general direction of travel, given his familiarity with the terrain and landscape of the property. By his best estimate they were headed more or less southeast and when they'd finally stopped, he guessed they had gone maybe a hundred and thirty yards. That would put them on or very close to the neighbor's, Corey Barker's private road. Apparently, they'd parked their vehicle on that secluded road to keep it hidden from public view.

With that pillow case over his head, he was provided only audible clues concerning their fury upon returning to their vehicle. But soon enough it became evident from all of the frustrated shouts and swearing that someone had shoved a pointed rod into the grill and punctured the radiator while they were away from the vehicle, as well as letting the air out of all four tires.

"You're all wasting your time with me," Dugan informed them. "Jessica left me days ago and I have no clue where she is or where she went – no clue at all. You can't beat out of me information that I don't have."

The pillow case provided no padding whatsoever to mitigate the blow of the gun butt to his head. "Then we'll just beat your ass for the fun of it."

"Your red neck hillbilly buddies who screwed with our ride just better hope we don't run into them out here," another one of them said.

"Corey Barker," Dugan said with the side of his face still numb from the blow. "He's not my 'buddy', just my neighbor. I'm pretty sure we're on his property. He's an old Vietnam War vet and I learned a while back how he's not all that fond of trespassers."

"The dumbass should've posted some signs on his property then."

Dugan heard the faint *swishhhh* followed very quickly by a soft thud, and then the series of swear words yelled in anguish.

"What the…? An *arrow?* He shot me with an arrow!!! Where is that son of a bitch?"

"It came from over there in those trees!"

Thwapppp! "Oh hell, now there's a damned arrow in my leg!!!"

Dugan heard the rustling of men scrambling, presumably to take defensive positions. He didn't move, and there was no longer any tension on the rope around his neck.

"I can't see squat over there," one of them complained. "He can't be more than fifty meters from here, somewhere in those trees but I can't see him yet. I'll try to get him in my sights."

"Phelps has that arrow sticking through his arm and it looks pretty bad, and now the LT's hit in the leg. Sgt. Miller, you and I can rush this bastard, he can't get us *all* with just a frickin' bow and a few arrows. We'll be two fast moving targets - create some confusion for him."

"Roger that - just need a tiny glimpse of this hill jack to get a shot – just one shot's all I need. When we rush him, he'll have to move to draw his bow and then we'll spot him! On your signal..."

Thwapppp! "Oh crap!!!" *Thwapppp!* Gasp...

Now he's over *there!* How'd he get all the way over there so fast? Gotta be more than just one dude out there with a bow."

Thwapppp! "Awe, son of a… Now I've got one right in my goddamned shoulder!!!"

Despite all the yelling there seemed to be a pause in the action when presumably all four men were stuck with arrows and none were all too eager to expose themselves to more arrows.

But the arrows had apparently now stopped flying finally, for *now*. Dugan heard mumbling and car doors opening. He heard what sounded like somebody dragging somebody else to the vehicle, and then groans and more cursing as the wounded men struggled climbing aboard the vehicle. He was close enough to the vehicle to hear their banter.

"Guys, these arrows have hunting broadheads on them so don't anyone even attempt pulling them out, not yet anyway – we'll cut the shafts first."

"Nobody will ever get all the blood cleaned out of this Jeep."

"They can just scrap it for parts. They owe us a new Wrangler anyway."

"Who's got enough water left in his canteen to dump into that radiator? Looks like it's a slow leak - we might make it to Operations if we have enough water. We can drive it slowly on its rims."

"Lieutenant Briggs is losing a lot of blood. His bandage is thoroughly soaked already."

"This totally sucks. I never figured how bad it actually hurts to have an arrow in part of my body before, but… It seems at least one of us nearly always needs a medic on these assignments."

"Hell, we *all* need medics this time!"

"What should we do with Randall?"

"Screw Randall! Leave him to his psycho hillbilly neighbors to worry about for now. We'll just have to catch up with him later."

A moment later the vehicle's ignition started with a hissing sound under the hood and then the rubber of four flat tires slapped the dirt road as it motored away.

Then once again the woods were quiet. Dugan wondered how his reclusive neighbor (or maybe he and some his old combat buddies) had managed to launch so many arrows so quickly (and so accurately) while staying safely hidden from view. Dugan hadn't heard a single gunshot, only the sound of arrows hitting their targets in rapid succession. *I never had any idea that the old guy could possibly be that skilled in archery and Ninja tactics.*

A moment later he heard footsteps crunching pine needles, approaching him. Even though he realized he could sure use his neighbor's help right now, Dugan wasn't particularly looking forward to seeing Corey Barker. Their last encounter hadn't been the most pleasant experience, as he recalled. Maybe the cranky old fart actually had a good side after all?

The duct tape was peeled off of Dugan's wrists and the pillow case yanked of his head. When he looked up to see the figure wearing the leafy bow hunter's camouflage, he was stunned to discover it wasn't his neighbor at all, but it was Jessica. She had a camouflage-painted recurve take-down bow slung over her shoulder with a camo quiver still half-full with camo-painted hunting arrows.

"Jessie? That was *you* doing all that? Wow! You're the last person in the world I ever expected to see out here this morning! I didn't even think I would ever see you again."

"Does that mean you're glad to see me?"

"Ha! You're a mind reader, what do you think?"

"I'm so sorry I left you, Dugan. It was a foolish thing I did. I know that now. You *will* forgive me, won't you?"

"Well, you did come back. And you freed me from these guys and their little interrogation session they had planned for me. And you're here with me right now. So yes, I forgive you. You won't ever leave me again though, right?"

"No, I won't. I will never ever leave you again, Dugan, for as long as I live. So, I guess you're stuck with me forever."

He suddenly felt the strongest urge to smile and he couldn't hide it. With his hands now freed Dugan loosened the rope noose and lifted it over his head before tossing it onto the ground. He looked at Jessica, and he still struggled to believe his own eyes that were telling him she was right here, and she was real. He glanced up at her bow.

"That was some impressive shooting you were doing."

"You know you taught me how. I bought this thirty-pound-draw recurve yesterday at a bow pro shop in Fayetteville. They have an indoor range just like in your barn and they have you try some bows before you buy one. They were pretty impressed with my shooting - they practically begged me to join their shooting team, but I politely declined."

"Oh yeah, I'll bet they were indeed impressed. And you're psychic, so you knew these guys would be here this morning, and you came prepared."

She nodded, "I did – I got the ice pick at a hardware store for their radiator, and that bow and those arrows plus the camouflage attire at that bow shop. I had a premonition about it two days ago."

"That was risky what you did. Those guys aren't regular Army - they're most likely Special Ops guys with special skills, hired as mercenaries for this job. The situation could have gotten out of control real fast."

"I know it could have. But it *didn't*."

"No, it didn't. Thank God it didn't! That bow hunter camo is pretty amazing – blends in perfectly with these trees, but how'd you manage to move without any of them spotting you?"

"I knew where their visual focus would be directed with each one of them before they focused – I was able to anticipate exactly where they'd be looking and I used economy of movement, tried to avoid disturbing any branches and kept behind the vegetation as much as possible."

"Well it worked - very impressive for sure."

"You don't think any of those arrow wounds will be life threatening, do you?"

"Well I had a sack over my head the whole time so I didn't get to see their wounds – from what they said it didn't sound like you hit any vitals. You could've used target arrows instead of hunting arrows to inflict less damage I suppose. I heard one of them mention that. But if they can control their bleeding and get themselves treated for shock soon enough they should all survive."

"I honestly do hope they'll be okay. I wasn't aiming to kill anyone but the things they were planning to do to you are unthinkable. I aimed for their arms and legs because I only wanted to get them to leave you alone and that's all."

"You sure did that all right. And I'm grateful that you did that. It looks like this kind of adventure will be a regular part of my life from now on, at least for the foreseeable future, just like it's been yours for so long. I guess I better start getting used to it, right?"

"You'll never get used to it completely I'm afraid."

"No, I don't suppose I ever will completely. So, what do you see up ahead for us in that crystal ball of yours?"

"I heard a news story on the radio yesterday. It was about a little farming community down in Mexico whose residents are being routinely harassed by a mafia-type gang. I guess it's basically just an isolated village that primarily grows maize and beans.

"So, this gang recently migrated from Mexico City to the quiet little community and it's been extorting money from the locals who barely earn enough from their crop harvests to survive already. It imposes its own 'tax' on these poor people, with the threat of murdering their family members if they fail to pay. It's a small community so the issue is not exactly a high priority for the Mexican government that is already struggling with a myriad of larger challenges. And the locals are simple third-world farmers who lack the resources or law enforcement infrastructure to remove this menace on their own. I think they could use our help."

"You'll have to teach me how to speak Spanish."

"That won't be any problem."

A spontaneous gust of warm wind suddenly brushed through the surrounding tree branches and swept over Dugan and Jessica, massaging their senses like a fresh reminder of the unpredictability of the natural world. And then as unexpectedly as it had stirred up it completely vanished and the air was once again as still as it had been, leaving no physical trace afterwards of its occurrence save a few leaves and pine needles that it had dislodged and carried to the forest floor, and the memory of it in the minds of two people.

This mysterious aspect of life and all of its experiences - just like a spontaneous wind - stirred in Dugan's consciousness all of a sudden like it never had before. He looked at Jessica now and savored her image, reminded that the prospect of never being able to see her again had dominated his thoughts throughout the last several days until literally only moments ago.

"I can't explain with words, Jessie, how glad I really am that you came back."

Made in United States
Troutdale, OR
01/15/2024